Francesca lau

And then, to Tessa's ~~~~~~~~~~ ~~~ the young girl whispering in her ear, 'It's time everybody stopped treating my dad as if he was made of Dresden china!'

'No likelihood I would ever do that!' Tessa whispered back. 'On duty I'll make a few concessions to his exalted station, but off duty he'll have to take his chance with the rest of them.'

'What are you two giggling about?' Max asked.

Tessa gave him a disarming smile. 'Women's talk—you wouldn't understand.'

For a moment she thought he was going to tick her off and then, suddenly, like the sun appearing from behind a cloud, she saw him smile, in a sensuous, definitely appealing kind of way. What a pity he didn't smile more often!

Margaret Barker pursued a variety of interesting careers before she became a full-time author. Besides holding a BA degree in French and Linguistics, she is a Licentiate of the Royal Academy of Music, a State Registered Nurse and a qualified teacher. Happily married, she has two sons, a daughter, and an increasing number of grandchildren. She lives with her husband in a sixteenth-century thatched house near the East Anglian coast.

ONE IN
A MILLION

BY
MARGARET BARKER

MILLS & BOON®

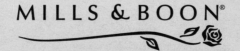

First published in Great Britain 1999
Harlequin Mills & Boon Limited,
Eton House, 18-24 Paradise Road, Richmond, Surrey TW9 1SR

© Margaret Barker 1999

ISBN 0 263 81761 X

Set in Times Roman 10½ on 11¾ pt.
03-9908-50842-D

Printed and bound in Spain
by Litografia Rosés S.A., Barcelona

CHAPTER ONE

'YOU don't remember me, do you?'

'Should I?'

Tessa looked up into the cool, expressionless, brown eyes and felt a shiver of dismay run down her spine. It wasn't the fact that Max Forster had forgotten her. Fourteen years had flashed by since she'd first known him.

The new obstetrics consultant had been working here on Nightingale Ward for a whole week, but because of his austere manner it was only today that Tessa had plucked up courage to speak to him on a personal level.

She'd recognised him, of course. With his tall, distinguished figure, he wasn't the sort of man who'd be forgotten in a hurry. He was handsome in a rugged sort of way and still young-looking in spite of the silvery white threads which the passing years had sprinkled liberally in his dark hair. At first glance, Max Forster had changed very little.

What dismayed Tessa was the expression, or rather lack of expression, in his eyes. When she'd babysat for his two-year-old daughter all those years ago, she'd been struck by the warmth and vitality that had radiated from the young father's face. It had been blatantly obvious that he'd enjoyed every moment of his life.

But this man in the expensive grey, pin-striped suit, frowning down at her as he folded up his stethoscope, looked as if life was simply passing him by.

She'd watched him as he'd examined their newly admitted patient. Oh, he'd been courteous and had answered Josie

Hargreaves's questions, but the moment the examination was over all his animation had seemed to disappear.

He'd been a newly qualified, carefree young house surgeon when she'd first known him. Was this what becoming a consultant had done to him? Had he become so high and mighty that he didn't want to talk to his obstetrics sister about anything other than work?

Tessa didn't think so. Max Forster's character couldn't have changed so radically. There must be some other reason.

'Are you going to move those curtains, Sister?' came a plaintive voice from the bed. 'I want to be able to see what's going on in the rest of the ward. If I'm going to be imprisoned here for another four months I'll need plenty of stimulation.'

Tessa smiled down at her patient. 'I doubt you'll go to full term, Josie. We're hoping the babies will be big enough to be delivered at about eight months, aren't we, Mr Forster?'

Max Forster nodded gravely. 'If you keep to the routine we've outlined, then an early delivery should be possible, Mrs Hargreaves.'

Their patient ran a hand through her greying, auburn hair. 'You mean you'll give me a whole month's reprieve? Wow! Well, I promise to stay in bed and rest if it means I'll go home sooner with my three babies. This is my last-ditch attempt at a family and with my history of miscarriages we can't take any chances, can we?'

'Absolutely not!'

Tessa swished away the curtains from around her patient's bed. Max Forster had moved to stand beside her as he handed over Josie's medical charts.

'Should I remember you, Sister?' she heard him say.

She started replacing the charts in the holder at the foot of the bed.

'I babysat for your daughter,' she told him, her head bowed over the charts. 'But it was a long time ago. No reason for you to remember me.'

As she began to walk down the ward she was wishing she hadn't spoken out of turn! She was aware that Mr Forster had quickened his step until he was once more at her side.

'If you wouldn't mind telling me your first name, Sister Grainger, perhaps I—'

'My name's Tessa. I was sixteen and I babysat a few times when you and Mrs Forster went out. It was just before you went to the States.'

They had reached the end of the ward. Her tummy was rumbling as it always did when she hadn't had time for breakfast. Should she offer the new consultant coffee and biscuits in her office? Her mother's home-made oat cakes might break the ice!

It was normal procedure with the other two consultants. In fact she often thought they timed their rounds to coincide with her elevenses routine.

'Would you like a coffee, Mr Forster? I usually—'

'Thank you. A cup of coffee would be much appreciated, Sister.'

He was looking down at her from his great height, his eyes quizzical.

'I think I remember you. There was a blonde-haired schoolgirl who used to help us out occasionally. Did you have long hair?'

She gave him a wary smile. 'Yes. I've only just had it cut…for my thirtieth birthday, actually.'

She pushed open the door to her office. Staff Nurse Anne Reeves jumped up guiltily, setting her coffee cup down on the small table.

'I was just going, Sister.'

Tessa smiled. Small, dark-haired Anne Reeves was a very competent staff nurse and worked hard on the ward. Recently engaged to a local teacher, she had assured Tessa that she intended to stay on at Moortown General after her marriage in the summer.

Since being appointed Sister of Nightingale Ward six months ago Tessa had been impressed by the skills of her nursing staff and she didn't mind if her trained staff took an extra couple of minutes on their coffee-break. It meant that they recharged their batteries so that they could give extra care and attention to their patients.

'Staff Nurse Williams could do with some help on the dressings round,' Tessa said, as Anne Reeves swished her cup under the tap, before making for the door.

'Is this your first Sister's post?' Max Forster asked, tossing a nursing magazine on to the floor as he settled himself into one of the well-worn, battered, but comfortable armchairs.

His long, grey-trousered legs seemed to stretch over half the room. Tessa stepped gingerly over them as she reached for the coffee-pot.

'My first Sister's post at Moortown General,' Tessa replied, as she poured out two cups of coffee and handed one to Max Forster. 'Sugar, milk?'

He shook his head. 'Black, please.'

'Can I tempt you to one of my mother's home-made oat cakes?'

She held the plate in front of him.

'I never…'

He paused and looked down at the plate, weighing it up solemnly as if it were a biopsy section from a surgical operation. 'It's a long time since I had an oat cake. Thank you, Sister.'

He was being studiously polite. She curbed her normally

garrulous tongue and waited for him to speak again. Sneaking a sureptitious sideways glance, she decided that he seemed to be enjoying the oat cake. Seconds ticked by until at last he broke the awkward silence.

'So, where were you before you worked here, Sister?'

With a sense of relief she launched into a brief résumé of her career.

'After I'd trained here at Moortown General, I wanted to move away from Yorkshire and see the bright lights of the city. So I staffed at St Celine's in London. Then I got a Sister's post in a small maternity hospital in north London. I loved the work there, but the hospital had to close.'

She took another sip of coffee. 'Suddenly, the bright lights didn't seem bright any more, if you know what I mean.'

She was trying to lighten the mood, make him unbend a little—if that was possible! She was rewarded by a brief twitching of the lips which could have been the beginning of a smile except that the eyes remained steadfastly solemn.

'So you decided to return to Yorkshire.'

She leaned back in her chair. 'Yes. I was beginning to realise that I'd had enough of London. I wanted to get back to my roots; walk over the moors, climb a few fells—'

She broke off, aware that he was actually looking interested in her conversation. Was the ice beginning to melt?

'I know the feeling,' he said quietly. 'There were many times when I longed to come back from the States to Yorkshire. We've taken a house in Cragdale.'

He paused for a moment, his eyes staring straight ahead as if in some private memory, before adding, 'Near where we used to live.'

Tessa smiled. 'We call Cragdale the Moortown General dormitory now because so many medical staff live over there. I'm hoping to be able to buy a small cottage near the river. The people who are selling it are caught in the dreaded house chain but I'm in no hurry. I live in the nurses' home when I'm on duty and spend my off-duty time at my parents' farm in Riversdale.'

'I remember driving our babysitter back to Riversdale,' he said quietly. 'Difficult to believe you're the grown-up version of that young schoolgirl.'

He was scrutinising her now, his lips pursed, his brow furrowed in concentration. 'Yes, I do remember you. If I imagine that long blonde hair that you used to flick out of your eyes, add the school uniform and—'

'And ignore the wrinkles of advancing age on my forehead,' she put in quickly, feeling suddenly very vulnerable at being the object of his scrutiny.

'Huh! Advancing age at thirty! You're still a child!'

'I sometimes wish I were! How's Francesca?'

He almost smiled and Tessa could see the thought of his daughter gave him pleasure.

'She's fine; in the sixth form at Moortown School.'

'I'd love to see her again. And how's Mrs Forster? I remember thinking she was the most beautiful woman I'd ever met. She always used to leave me a tray of food even though I'd already had my supper at home. And being sixteen and permanently starving I used to—'

She broke off. 'Excuse me, sir, while I answer the phone.'

Reaching for the ringing phone on her desk, she spoke quickly. 'Sister Grainger here... Why, yes, of course, Mr Delaware. I'll tell him at once.'

It was only as she put down the phone that she noticed the pallor which had crept over Max Forster's face. Had she said something to upset him?

'That was Mr Simon Delaware. You asked him to call you when he was free to discuss that difficult case. He said you would know what he—'

'Yes, yes of course,' he said, dismissively, as he made for the door. 'Thank you for the coffee, Sister.'

'Give my regards to Mrs Forster. Perhaps—'

He turned at the door and interrupted her. 'I would if it were possible but Francesca and I are on our own now.'

The door slammed shut. She swallowed hard. Oh, God, why had she assumed that everything would be the same after fourteen years when so many marriages ended prematurely? But the Forsters had been the perfect couple.

To her sixteen-year-old impressionable mind they'd seemed the epitome of what a happily married couple should be. The Forster house had been full of laughter and fun. She vividly remembered one summer evening when Max Forster had called to ask if she could do a few hours' babysitting.

She'd readily agreed because she'd loved going to the Forsters' house. They'd been generous when paying her and little Francesca had rarely woken up, so she'd been able to do her homework, have a change of scenery, a tasty supper and get paid for it!

Max Forster had collected her in his open topped sports car. It had been exhilarating, driving from Riversdale over the moors, slowing down only when a sheep strayed into the road. He'd chatted to her all the time, making her laugh as he'd recounted some of the baby things that Francesca had said. As he'd driven her down into Cragdale she remembered having thought that when she was grown up she would like to marry a man like Max Forster.

And later, as she'd looked out of the window and had seen Max and Catherine returning from their evening out, their arms around each other's waists as they'd left the car, she'd felt so happy that the Forsters seemed to have had everything. If ever a marriage had been made in heaven, it had been this one.

But not any more, apparently. That might account for the

change in Max's personality because she couldn't believe he would have instigated the split with Catherine. He'd absolutely doted on her.

'Could you come and have a word with Milly Baxter, Sister?'

Anne Reeves poked her head round the door.

'She's having a difficult time persuading baby Jonathan to feed. She said you had a special way of dealing with him that works like magic.'

Tessa smiled. 'I wouldn't call it magic. More like common sense. I'm on my way, Anne.'

Milly Baxter was red-faced and flustered when Tessa arrived in her curtained-off cubicle.

'It's hopeless, Sister. I thought after you helped me yesterday I wouldn't have any more problems but we're back to square one again today.'

Tessa leaned down and lifted the tiny, squalling baby from his mother and patted him gently over her shoulder. Obligingly, the little scrap gave a loud burp and stopped crying.

'Well, would you believe it?' the young mother said. 'That's what I've been trying to do for the past ten minutes but he's determined to show everybody what a hopeless mum I am.'

'You've had a difficult time, Milly,' Tessa said gently. 'It's only five days since your Caesarean operation and only two days since you started breast-feeding.'

Milly ran a hand over her tousled brown hair. 'Yes, but when I was expressing my breast milk for the nurses to feed Jonathan with I had no problem. There's plenty of milk there for him so why doesn't he just get on with it instead of—'

'Now, you mustn't worry, Milly,' Tessa said, sitting down on the side of the bed, the baby snuggled in the crook of one arm and the other around her patient's shoulders. 'Just tickle Jonathan's lips with your finger like this... Go on...you try...'

Tentatively, Milly copied Tessa's movements.

'Now hold him against you; snuggle him up to your breast. Don't worry, I'm holding his bottom, he can't fall...there! What did I tell you!'

'Ah, just listen to him, Sister. He sounds as if he was starving, poor lamb. But I don't think I can get him to latch on like that by myself. Will you help me with the next feed?'

'I'll try, but if I'm tied up with a difficult delivery or something I'll ask one of the nurses to help you. You'll soon get the hang of it. It's the most natural thing in the world.'

There was a rustle of the curtains and Tessa looked up to find Simon Delaware reading the charts at the end of the bed. Milly was one of his patients.

As Nightingale Ward had been expanded recently, there were now three consultants. Simon Delaware was the most senior, followed by Carl Devine who'd been appointed from senior registrar about a year ago and the newly appointed Max Forster.

Tessa stood up. 'Are you here to do a round, sir?'

Simon Delaware shook his head. 'No, but I'd like a word with you, Sister, when you've finished helping Milly.'

She smiled down at her patient. 'I think you can cope on your own now, can't you, Milly?'

Her patient nodded. 'I'll be OK till the next time.'

Mr Delaware moved to the patient's side and touched the infant's cheek.

'Jonathan's filling out nicely, Milly. You don't need to worry about him. How are you feeling?'

'A lot better since Sister persuaded him to feed.'

'I'll be back later,' Tessa said, going out through the curtains.

Simon Delaware followed, walking down the ward and out into the corridor that led to the prenatal section of Nightingale with her.

'How are you getting on with Max Forster?' he asked, in a casual voice.

'Fine! Why do you ask?'

'I just wondered if you found him a bit difficult to hold a conversation with. I didn't notice it when he came for his interview because he's a very talented, experienced obstetrician and he was very fluent when discussing his subject. But trying to get through to him on a social level...'

He paused, looking down at her with a puzzled expression. 'I mean, it must be years since his wife died so you'd think he'd have got over it by now, wouldn't you?'

Tessa felt a lump rising in her throat. The beautiful Catherine Forster had died? Oh, God, she couldn't imagine anything more awful!

'I'm not sure if he would have got over it,' she said carefully. 'When I knew them it was obvious they were very much in love.'

She pushed open the door of her office. Simon Delaware followed her inside and leaned against her desk.

'Yes, my wife mentioned that you'd told her you knew the Forsters years ago. That's absolutely perfect from my point of view.'

She frowned. 'What do you mean?'

She'd just had a most terrible shock and Simon Delaware, normally a very sympathetic man, was telling her that knowing the Forsters was perfect.

'Sorry—that must sound callous. Let me explain. I've decided to invite Max Forster over for the evening to try and break the ice. Hannah's all for it. We've got to do something to draw him out of himself. When I asked him just now he refused. Said he didn't go out much—didn't like to leave his daughter on her own. Do you know how old she is?'

'I used to babysit her fourteen years ago so she must be fifteen or sixteen now.'

'Definitely old enough to be left! What I wanted to ask you, Tessa, was if you'd come to supper and persuade Max to come with you. What do you think?'

'I'm not sure.'

She sat down at her desk, automatically rearranging the case notes of the new admissions which someone had recently delivered.

'I mean I don't think I'll be any more successful than you if he wants to keep an iron curtain around himself…unless…'

'Yes?'

'Unless you were to invite his daughter, Francesca, to come along as well. She might enjoy a night out.'

Simon Delaware grinned. 'A night out with the wrinklies, you mean?'

'Speak for yourself!'

She put a hand over her mouth and then laughed as she saw the consultant's happy expression. This was another man who'd found the perfect partner and married her.

His wife, Dr Hannah Morgan, had been senior registrar when Simon Delaware had married her four years ago. Hannah now worked part time in Obstetrics Outpatients and she and Tessa had become firm friends. On a couple of occasions she'd been invited over to the Delawares' lovely house by the river in Cragdale.

Simon Delaware glanced at his watch. 'Must dash! Can I leave you to arrange it?'

Tessa gave him a wry smile. 'I'll do my best, but I can't promise that Mr Forster will agree. Even in his younger days he seemed like a man who knew his own mind. How old is he now?'

'Forty. Hardly the time to go into a permanent state of hibernation. But everyone I've spoken to says he puts out signals that he's not interested in forming relationships, even discouraging people who simply want to be friendly acquaintances.'

She took a deep breath. 'Do you know anything about Mrs Forster's death?'

Simon Delaware's brow furrowed. 'I believe it was a tragic accident, but I don't know any details.'

Tessa shivered. 'How horrible!'

'So we're going to have to approach him in a very sympathetic way, Tessa.'

'I know. It makes it worse now that you've told me…' She swallowed hard. 'But I'll give it my best shot.'

It hadn't been easy. As Tessa looked around the assembled company in Simon Delaware's large sitting room she felt more than a twinge of sympathy for the man she'd coerced into attending this specifically-designed-to-draw-him-out gathering.

Simon and Hannah's pyjama-clad children, three-year-old Jamie and two-year-old Gwen, were toddling around between the occasional tables, holding out bowls of nuts and crisps to the guests who were still standing in a group in front of the log fire.

Tessa eyed the squashy sofas and chairs longingly, wondering how long it would be before people started relaxing into them. She'd had a long, tiring day on Nightingale and would have preferred a hot bath and an early night.

Looking tentatively sideways at Max Forster as he toyed with a glass of wine, she decided that he probably felt the same as she did!

Nobody had fully switched off and the main topic of conversation was still medical. Adam and Trisha Redman, a charming couple who were in charge of the fertility clinic in nearby Bramdale, were discussing the importance of pre-natal rest for their high risk patients.

They were both doctors and managed to combine their professional work with looking after their children, eased by the fact that they occupied family living quarters at the clinic.

'It's so awful for the patient when she's gone through a long period of fertility treatment,' Trisha was saying in an impassioned voice, 'and then a few weeks into the pregnancy she loses the baby because she wasn't getting enough rest.'

'Well, don't worry, Trisha,' Tessa said. 'I agree entirely with you that these potential mothers should rest. We've got Josie Hargreaves, the mother with the unborn triplets you sent us, safely tucked up in bed.'

'Which is where these two should be,' Simon Delaware said, reaching down to scoop up his son and daughter, one under each arm.

'Can Michael read me a story?' little Jamie said as he was carried out through the door.

'Just one and then you've got to go to sleep,' Simon told him.

Tessa smiled. Hannah had told her that Jamie loved Michael. Jamie's eleven-year-old half-brother was Simon's son from his first disastrous marriage. It was good when a couple found happiness the second time around.

She glanced at Francesca, who was clutching a glass of orange juice and giving polite, dutiful answers to the questions that Phil Dixon, recently appointed houseman on Nightingale, was firing at her.

Phil was the only other person who was under thirty.

Tessa surmised that Simon and Hannah had invited him to make up the numbers as soon as they knew that Francesca had been persuaded to attend.

Phil was an intense young man and Tessa sensed that Francesca was finding him extremely uninspiring. Discussing the necessity of getting good grades in her biology and chemistry exams if she intended to be a doctor, it was obviously not Francesca's idea of a fun night out!

'Why don't we all sit down?' Hannah, the perfect hostess, said, sinking into one of the armchairs.

Tessa flashed her a grateful smile as she made for the sofa. Max and Francesca, managing to shake off Phil, gravitated towards Tessa, one on either side. It was as if, because she'd instigated their attendance here, they were holding her responsible for preventing them from having an evening doing whatever it was they chose to do!

She remembered the embarrassing conversation she'd had with Max last week when she'd put forward the idea that he might enjoy Simon's and Hannah's dinner party. He'd insisted that he didn't socialise because he had a duty to take care of his daughter. Relentlessly, she'd pointed out that Simon and Hannah would be delighted if Francesca went along as well.

That had been the turning point! He'd frowned, pursed his lips, turned on his heel and muttered that he'd think about it. Meeting up with Hannah in Obstetrics Outpatients, she'd been delighted to hear that Max had finally phoned her and accepted the invitation.

'My daughter's been trying hard to remember you but she's drawn a blank, haven't you, Francesca?' Max said quietly, leaning forward so that he could look at his daughter on the other side of Tessa.

Francesca, brown-eyed like her father but with the captivating, long, blonde hair of her mother gave a vivacious smile, revealing perfectly formed, white teeth.

'I don't remember being two. In fact, I don't remember anything that happened to me before the age of four, not even—'

She broke off, her lovely face clouding. Reaching across in front of Tessa, she put a hand over her father's. 'It's OK, Daddy, I'm not going to...'

Only Tessa saw the strained look on Max's face and the almost imperceptible shake of his head.

'It's a pity I don't remember you,' Francesca rushed on, her voice deliberately light. 'Was I difficult to handle?'

Tessa smiled. 'You were asleep most of the time. But I do remember that there was one night when you wouldn't settle so I took you down by the fire, made you some hot chocolate and read you a story. By the time your mother and father got back you were fast asleep in my arms.'

She deliberately missed out the bit about having to change Francesca's night-time nappy. That sort of information could be terribly embarrassing to a sixteen-year-old.

'Now you mention it, I remember that occasion,' Max said in a far-away voice.

He put the tips of his fingers together and studied them with an air of intense concentration as he spoke.

'Yes, that was the night I had to carry Francesca upstairs, and when I came down Catherine had gone out to drive Tessa home. I used to worry about her driving at night on the narrow country lanes round here. My nerves were on edge until she got back. Catherine wasn't a good driver.'

He dropped his hands into his lap. 'Strange how memories suddenly come back to you.'

Tessa swallowed hard. Oh, God, this was going to be such a strain! Max looked as if he'd seen a ghost. Memories, flooding back, were not conducive to social gatherings especially when they were tied in with the tragic accident of the one you loved.

As Tessa took a sip of her wine she couldn't help wondering if Francesca had been about to divulge something about the incident that was responsible for her mother's death. The barely perceptible censorius gesture from her father had restrained her. Perhaps Francesca wanted to bring things out into the open, whereas Max preferred to keep his intense sorrow locked away.

If that was the case, Tessa was definitely on Francesca's side. From the brooding look on Max's face she realised that by keeping the tragedy inside him his real emotions were being slowly eaten away.

And yet he'd shown animation for a few brief seconds just now when he'd said he remembered the night when she'd had to spend time caring for the little, restless Francesca. His eyes had brightened up and the expressive look on his face had given her some hope that he wasn't entirely robotic!

But she told herself she mustn't try to shoulder his problems, taking them on as her own. On a social level he was only a passing acquaintance. He would have to work out his own salvation. At least young Francesca seemed a well-adjusted girl so Max had done a good job of parenting on his own.

The arrival of the final couple of guests livened up the party. Carl and Jenni Devine swept into the room, apologising for their late appearance.

'Sorry we're late, Hannah. Jack and Ann Hamilton are baby-sitting for us and it was difficult to get away. You know how Ann can talk!'

'Don't we all?'

There was a general chorus of agreement from around the room. Before she'd taken early retirement and married Sir

Jack Hamilton, who was chairman of the governors at Moortown General, Ann Gregson had been Sister in charge of Nightingale for many years.

Tessa remembered how she'd been scared stiff of Sister Gregson during her days as a student nurse but recently, meeting Ann Hamilton socially, she'd discovered what a charming woman she really was, with a heart of gold.

A smiling Jenni waved across the room to Tessa as she accepted a glass of wine from Hannah. Tessa waved back. It was always fun to see Jenni. Some time during the evening she hoped they'd have time for a long chat.

They had so much in common—both Tessa and Jenni had been born on farms in Riversdale and had attended the same local schools, before starting their nursing training at the Moortown General.

It was only after qualifying that they'd lost touch for a while. Jenni had taken over from Ann Gregson as Sister on Nightingale until starting her family. Now, with Tessa back at the hospital, they were catching up with each other's news.

Tessa had been delighted to find Jenni happily married to Carl Devine and the proud mother of twins. They lived in a house on the hill in Cragdale not too far from Riverside Cottage, the little house she was hoping to buy.

Hannah's invaluable housekeeper, Mrs Rainer, came bustling in, wiping her hands on her blue and white apron as she spoke to Hannah, before going back to the kitchen.

'Supper's ready so let's go into the dining room,' Hannah announced in a loud voice that carried above the conversational noise.

They were ten around the table. Once again Tessa found herself flanked by Max and Francesca. She was beginning to get used to it and found she was actually enjoying chatting to them so she experienced a pleasant warm glow when

Max lifted the starched, white, linen napkin from her plate and spread it over her lap.

'Would you like one of these Italian breadsticks, Sister?' he asked, holding a glass jar in front of her.

'I'd like one, please,' Francesca chimed in from the other side of Tessa, her hand outstretched in anticipation. 'I love them. I could eat the whole jar.'

Max smiled fondly. 'I wasn't asking you, Francesca,' he said in a teasing voice.

Looking at the smile on Max's face, Tessa thought it was the most expressive smile she'd ever seen and the most transforming.

From being a dour, obstinate, forty-something consultant, he had become a young-looking, interesting character with the potential to turn heads. Anyone who succeeded in captivating this man's heart for the second time around would be a lucky woman!

'Lucky' being the operative word. Because that particular scenario just wasn't likely to happen. She felt sure that Max Forster would continue to nurse his secret sorrow for ever. Even now, barely seconds after his smile, his expression had reverted to one of solemnity.

'They're only breadsticks,' she said lightly as she took one from the jar he was holding in front of her.

His brown eyes flickered. 'What do you mean?'

'You were looking at them as if they were objects of extreme importance,' she said, in the same teasing tone. 'As if they were something you were going to take to the path lab for analysis. Anyway, thank you. Your turn, Francesca. Don't take them all.'

Francesca laughed. 'Thanks, Tessa.'

And then to Tessa's amazement, she heard the young girl whispering in her ear, 'It's time everybody stopped treating my dad as if he was made of Dresden china!'

'No likelihood I would ever do that!' Tessa whispered back. 'On duty I'll make a few concessions to his exalted station, but off duty he'll have to take his chance with the rest of them.'

Francesca dissolved into a fit of the giggles.

'What are you two giggling about?' Max asked.

Tessa gave him a disarming smile. 'Women's talk—you wouldn't understand.'

For a moment she thought he was going to tick her off and then, suddenly, like the sun appearing from behind a cloud, she saw his expression change. And this time she could really appreciate the quality of the smile. It was sensuous...sort of sexy in a definitely appealing kind of way. What a pity he didn't smile more often!

She decided that Max Forster was a man who'd forgotten how to smile, who thought it wrong to enjoy himself...no, not wrong. It simply didn't occur to him that enjoyment was a necessary part of life.

Well, she was going to teach him otherwise! She had no idea why she'd suddenly decided to take this on as her personal crusade. She'd definitely decided that she didn't feel sorry for him. He had everything going for him in life if only he would reach out and grasp it.

What she couldn't understand were her own motives. Why did it seem so important that she recapture the old Max Forster she'd glimpsed all those years ago? Was it that she wanted him to realise his potential as a human being?

Deep down inside she had the sudden self-realisation that she wasn't being totally altruistic. There was more to it than that.

She cared, she really cared. But where would that lead her? Wouldn't it be better if she washed her hands of the project before she got too caught up in it?

Huge bowls of pasta and spaghetti were being passed

around the table. She realised that Max had been holding a bowl in front of her for several seconds while she mused.

'Thank you, Mr Forster,' she said, as she picked up the serving spoon and fork, endeavouring to coax the long strands onto her plate.

This was one of the social operations she found very difficult. It was impossible to take a small amount. As she attempted to separate six strands a whole colony threatened to land on her plate!

'Here, let me help you.'

Surprised by his concerned tone, she watched as Max put the bowl on the table and, with his sensitive, expert, surgeon's hands grasping the spoon and fork, deftly scooped up the small helping she had been chasing. As it landed on her plate she turned to him and smiled.

'Thank you, Mr Forster. I—'

'Do you think you could call me Max?'

'Only if you'll call me Tessa.'

Francesca was nudging her from the other side. 'Can I swap this spaghetti sauce for the wormy bits?'

Tessa and Francesca found themselves laughing hilariously as they negotiated the exchange of the serving bowls, not realising that the rest of the guests had suddenly stopped chattering.

'Shh!' Max whispered solemnly.

Francesca rolled her eyes in a mock grimace and Tessa had to stifle another giggle.

Hannah was standing up. 'Just a brief word. I wanted to invite everybody here tonight so that we can say welcome to our new consultant, Max, and his lovely daughter, Francesca. We all hope you're going to be happy here in Cragdale and at the hospital.'

Everybody had raised their wine glasses. 'To Max and Francesca!'

Tessa, glancing sideways, saw that Max's full, sensuous lower lip was quivering. He was obviously very touched by the united sentiments. She watched as he stood up, turning his head to look at each person in turn.

'Thank you all for making me feel so welcome. I have to say I had mixed feelings about coming here tonight. You see…'

Tessa saw the lip quivering again and as he swallowed hard she found herself holding her breath.

'You see, coming back to Moortown and Cragdale has brought back so many memories, most of them happy but some…too poignant to contemplate so…'

Tessa could see that he'd dried up in mid-sentence. This important, distinguished man who handled medical crises with such skill was, temporarily, at a loss for words.

She longed to speak on his behalf but knew it would be misconstrued. In an automatic gesture born of desperation she nudged Francesca. The young girl, realising what was required of her rose to her feet and beamed around the table.

'I'd just like to add my thanks to Daddy's. You've all been so helpful since we got back. I was born here in Cragdale, you know, and I think it's the greatest place on earth. And it's got some of the kindest people like our host and hostess, Hannah and Simon…and, er…'

Tessa was on her feet beside Francesca now, raising her glass and proposing that they all drink to Hannah and Simon.

The conversations were resumed again. Under cover of all the chattering, Tessa was suddenly aware that Max was speaking to her in a quiet voice.

'Thanks, Tessa.'

She put down her fork and turned to him.

'Thanks for what, Max?'

She'd deliberately added his name to reinforce the fact that they were both on first-name terms now.

His eyes were serious. 'For saving the day.'

'Oh, it wasn't that important.'

He reached out and covered her hand with his own. 'It was important to me. I don't know why I suddenly felt it impossible to go on speaking.'

'Perfectly natural,' Tessa said lightly. 'All these memories floating around now that you're back in this part of the world where you had such a happy life. It will be difficult for you to come to terms with the fact that you have to live here without Catherine.'

She paused, then added, 'Initially, it will be difficult but you'll get over it. Time is a great healer.'

She knew she'd stuck her neck out, treating him in the same way she would if he'd been one of her patients who needed pointing in the right direction.

A faint smile crossed his lips. 'Old Father Time hasn't done much healing in the past twelve years.'

'Maybe you didn't want him to.'

He looked startled at the way she'd spoken to him. Perhaps she'd gone too far!

Suddenly he dropped his head and spoke, almost to himself. 'Maybe I didn't.'

When he looked up again she saw that his eyes were bright and moist.

'Thanks for the consultation, Sister. Ever thought of taking up psychotherapy?' he added wryly.

She smiled. 'I prefer obstetrics. You get an excellent type of consultant in the business.'

He threw back his head and laughed. She was so amazed that she could feel her jaw dropping and she had to pull herself together because Francesca was asking what she'd said that was so funny.

'It wasn't really funny, Francesca. At least it wasn't meant to be. Oh, good, here comes the pudding. Hannah's brilliant on puddings. You must try the meringue baskets...'

She realised as she chattered on to Francesca that what she'd really been doing underneath all her concerned advice to Max had been flirting with him. And the thought that she actually wanted him to notice her as somebody other than Sister on Nightingale was very disturbing!

At what point had her intended psychotherapy turned into something that could be emotionally hazardous? She would have to be more careful in future...

CHAPTER TWO

'So how do you think my supper party went last week?' Hannah asked, handing Tessa a cup of coffee. 'Do you think we managed to chip away some of the ice surrounding Max?'

They were taking a couple of minutes off in their obstetric outpatients' schedule. Once a week Tessa spent part of the afternoon in Hannah's clinic, dealing with patients who were going to be admitted to Nightingale.

Hannah was a very competent and sympathetic doctor and Tessa found that the patients she'd first seen here in the clinic were always more relaxed and confident when they came to be admitted to Nightingale.

She took a sip of her coffee.

'I think it was a very successful evening. It certainly brought young Francesca out of her shell. Did you see how she got our young houseman, Phil Dixon, to discuss pop music by the end of the evening?'

She smiled as the amusing memories flooded back. 'She even made him dance with her when you cleared the floor in the sitting room and put on your latest trendy CDs.'

Hannah laughed. 'I hope you realise those trendy CDs were specially bought to liven up the occasion. We had to take advice from young Michael to find out what's in at the moment.'

She leaned across the desk towards Tessa. 'Yes, that was a sight for sore eyes. Serious, sober-sided Phil got more than he bargained for with Francesca, didn't he? But what about

Francesca's dad? I noticed you didn't attempt to drag Max onto the floor.'

Tessa cleared a space on Hannah's desk and put down her cup.

'Why on earth should I? The deal was for me to drag along the main characters and I did just that. That was the end of my responsibility so—'

She froze as she suddenly noticed the half-opened door and the tall, grey-suited figure, hovering on the threshold. How long had Max been there? How much had he heard?

Hannah had noticed him, too. She was already on her feet, smiling a welcome.

'Would you like coffee, Max? I think we can squeeze another cup from this cafetière.'

'Thanks, Hannah. I called in to review the surrogate twins case with you so it's fortunate that Sister…that Tessa's here as well.'

Max lowered himself onto one of the upright chairs reserved for patients. Tessa thought the chair appeared much too small for his muscular frame and he looked decidedly uncomfortable. He was also avoiding eye contact with her.

He must have heard what she'd said when he was coming in! Oh, God! After all her efforts to gain his trust at Hannah's house last week she'd gone and spoiled it with a few ill-chosen words. How much had he heard? Did he think she'd persuaded him to go to the party out of pity?

Well, that had been the initial idea. It had only been the time she'd spent with Max that had changed her attitude.

'The surrogate mother-to-be of the twins is due to see me in a few minutes,' Max was saying, in a studiously professional voice, 'so if Tessa could come along to meet her we could discuss her treatment.'

'Yes, that would be very useful,' Tessa said quickly. 'Could you fill me in on the details, Max?'

Oh, they were being so polite and professional with each other! It was as if she had never discussed anything other than obstetrics with this man. The fact that she thought she'd gained his confidence the other night no longer counted.

'The case notes are in my consulting rooms. You can read the details when you come along.'

Tessa had to suppress a shiver as she listened to Max's icy tone.

'Well, perhaps you could give me a brief outline,' she persisted.

He put down his coffee-cup and faced her for the first time, his veiled eyes giving no indication of his feelings.

'Samantha Jones and Jill Mason are sisters,' he began in a matter-of-fact tone. 'Samantha, the elder by two years, had a hysterectomy for cancer ten years ago. Now, aged thirty-five and newly married, she wants a family. Her sister Jill has been impregnated with Samantha's husband's sperm at the Bramdale Clinic and is expecting twins.'

He stood up. 'Thanks for the coffee, Hannah. If you'd like to follow me, Tessa…'

She turned in the doorway to catch Hannah's eye. Her friend was making a gesture of resignation and whispering, 'Don't worry. I don't think he heard.'

'I think he did,' Tessa whispered back, before hurrying to catch up with Max.

Oh, well, she must simply concentrate on her professional work now. Time enough to worry about her social obligations when she went off duty.

Staff Nurse Rona Phillips had already prepared the surrogate mother for examination when Tessa and Max arrived in his consulting room.

Rona had switched on the ultrasound scanning machine. Tessa watched as blurred images of the twins appeared on the screen.

Glancing sideways at Max, Tessa saw that he was looking pleased. Nothing like work to bring him out of himself!

'A healthy-looking pair of babies,' he was saying. 'I could safely tell you what sex they are if you like—or would you prefer to remain in the dark?'

'What do you want to do, Samantha?' Jill asked, raising her head from the couch to look at her sister who was seated beside her. 'They're your babies, not mine. I'm simply cooking them in my microwave.'

Samantha laughed as she took hold of her sister's hand.

'What do you think, Sis? Shall we find out? Yes, why not? To be honest, I don't mind what they are so long as they're healthy, but I know Bob is dying to know if he'll have someone to go with him to his football matches.'

Max leaned forward to scrutinise the screen. 'Well, in that case, Samantha, you can tell your husband he'll have to buy two extra tickets. They're both boys.'

Samantha grinned. 'Bob will be over the moon! Thanks, Doctor. Isn't that great Jill?'

Jill beamed happily at her excited sister. 'It's wonderful so long as your twins don't start playing football while they're still inside me!'

'We've got to make sure you stay healthy, Jill,' Max said, suddenly deadly serious again.

'Because of the fact that you miscarried during the first surrogate pregnancy, I'd like to admit you to Nightingale in a couple of weeks. We don't want to take any chances with this one. If you stay on at home, you won't get enough rest.'

'But I'll only be seven months, Mr Forster.'

Max smiled. 'Don't worry. We'll probably have to deliver you at eight months so four weeks in Nightingale won't be too bad, will it?'

'I'll visit you every day, Jill,' Samantha said. 'You can have bunches of grapes and boxes and boxes of chocolates.'

'Go easy on the chocolates,' Tessa put in quickly. 'One or two a day will be OK but beyond that...'

'The nurses can eat them,' Samantha said, her excitement at the prospect of being a mother making her as bubbly as a teenager.

'And don't worry about your children, Jill, or your precious husband, Mike. I'll take care of them while you're in hospital. They're only just round the corner from us, remember, and it will be good practice for when I've got my own babies.'

Jill gave a mock groan. 'My three little terrors will more likely put you off the whole idea.'

She grinned as she patted her swollen abdomen. 'That's why I'm going to find it so easy to hand over these two.'

'There's a good rapport between those sisters,' Tessa remarked to Max when their patients had gone. 'It's so important in these cases. Trisha and Adam vet their patients very carefully over at the Bramdale Fertility Clinic.'

Max nodded in agreement. 'Yes, Trisha and Adam seem to be doing a good job at their clinic. Another favourable factor about our two mothers is that they have the same auburn hair and hazel eyes.'

'Yes, I noticed that. Trisha and Adam made a note of that in the case history here.'

She was scanning the papers on Adam's desk.

'I always feel confident when Trish and Adam send us a surrogate mother. They do thorough checks on every aspect. If they're in any doubt about the rapport between the surrogate mother and the receiving mother they won't go ahead with the treatment.'

Max nodded gravely. 'I entirely agree with that approach. Rapport is everything, isn't it?'

She was sitting at the side of his desk, holding the case

notes that she'd been scanning. Something in his tone told her that he wasn't referring entirely to the case in hand. There was a double *entendre* hidden away somewhere in his remarks!

'Yes, it's important to get on with someone you're trying to help,' she said quietly.

His brown eyes flickered. 'And important that the help should be given with the right motives.'

So he *had* heard her caustic comments! She reached out across the desk and touched his arm. The smooth, expensive cloth seemed to burn her fingers and she felt a heightened colour rush to her face. An awful feeling of guilt spread through her.

'Max, I can explain. I—'

He moved his arm. 'There's nothing to explain. I understand perfectly. Since Catherine died I've been inundated with do-gooders all trying to—'

'I'm not a do-gooder!'

She realised that she'd actually stamped her foot, before going round the desk to stand looking down at him.

'I wanted to help you because you were a good friend I knew from a long time ago.'

He stood up so that he towered above her. She made to back off but he put both his hands on either side of her arms. She remained motionless, swallowing hard to disguise how disturbed she felt to be so near him.

His fingers tightened on her arms and she felt a frisson of something akin to excitement. Maybe this man didn't need any help after all!

'I know you wanted to help me as a friend,' he said slowly, his brown eyes now firmly holding her gaze.

She felt mesmerised as she watched his lips moving to enunciate the words. For the first time she noticed what strong, white teeth he had. And she felt drawn to watch his tongue as it moved up and down…

She must concentrate on what he was saying! If only he would take his hands from the side of her arms she would be able to think more clearly.

'You're not the only person to have tried to help me like this,' he was explaining, his voice expressive and impassioned.

'Over the last twelve years I've been overwhelmed with social invitations so I guessed you'd been coerced into dragging me along to Hannah and Simon's.'

She dropped her eyes, studiously fixing them on the case notes that were stacked on the desk.

'I'm sorry I used those words,' she said quietly.

At last he'd removed his hands from her arms! She dared to meet his intense gaze again, even though for some unknown reason her heart was thumping madly.

He raised his hand and put one long, well-manicured, tapering finger under her chin, tilting her face towards his.

'The words weren't important,' he said huskily. 'It was the motivation that I objected to. It was the same old story that I've had to get used to. It's called, let's bring Max out of his shell and get him back in circulation.'

'Max, I—'

'Oh, I've always gone along with it, gone through the motions of pretending I was unaware what was happening, but—'

'If I'd known how you felt I—'

'Hey! Don't get so worried!'

She felt a rush of relief that his tone had become so light-hearted. He was actually smiling now as he continued in the same, easygoing manner.

'I didn't mean to upset you like this, Tessa. You did the dutiful deed you were asked to do and—'

'I'm glad you understand that I was in a difficult position.'

She took a deep breath to steady her nerves. 'But I would really like to help you, Max.'

Gently, he put his arms out and pulled her towards him. She realised it was a friendly gesture, the gesture of an old friend, a sort of brotherly—or fatherly gesture. Whatever! But she told herself defensively that it wasn't meant to be sensual.

She remained very still, trying to calm herself, but the smooth texture of his jacket against her chin was decidedly unnerving. She tried to think of him in the way she had when she'd babysat for his little daughter all those years ago, but it was impossible.

'Forget about helping me, Tessa,' he said quietly. 'I long ago decided I was immune to all these well-intentioned advances designed to change my life. My life doesn't need changing. I'm perfectly happy with my work. And I've got Francesca for company at home.'

He released her from his friendly embrace and she almost gave a sigh of relief. Feeling his body so close to hers, it had been overwhelmingly disturbing. She looked up at him but he seemed unmoved. Over the past twelve years, had he totally switched off all real emotion?

She leaned against the side of his desk. 'So, have you decided you enjoy a monk-like existence?'

He half opened his mouth as his eyes registered amazement. She really had gone too far this time! What on earth had made her say that? It was as if her lips had a mind of their own. But her curiosity had got the better of her. Mentally, she cringed as she waited for his expected retort.

He raised an eyebrow. 'You don't mince your words, do you?'

'I'm sorry, I—'

'Oh, don't apologise! I like a girl who speaks her own mind. Well, for your information, I certainly haven't lived like a monk since Catherine died. I have a physical hunger just like any other healthy man and—'

'Oh, please, I wasn't prying. I—'

He reached forward and took both her hands in his. She found she welcomed the warmth of his skin against her own as she raised her eyes to his.

'Don't worry, Tessa. I wasn't going to give you a blow-by-blow account of my sex life.'

She decided that the rakish grin that was spreading over his face was definitely enhancing his good looks. She caught her breath as she realised the last thing she wanted to know was that Max had enjoyed a sex life. For some unknown reason, she knew she would have preferred to think that he'd been totally abstemious during the last twelve years.

Now, why did she feel like that? With a sinking heart she realised that she had strange feelings akin to jealousy when she thought of the women he might have slept with.

Carefully, she extracted her hands from his grasp and moved back to the other side of the desk. He was watching her, a faint, enigmatic smile on his lips.

What must he be thinking about her? She'd patronised him at the supper party, dispensing her homespun theories about how to forget the past and get on with living a full life. But in reality, underneath his serious demeanour, Max had got his life sorted out and totally under control.

Obviously, there would be no shortage of women who would enjoy a physical relationship with him. He was a highly desirable man. Even as she sat there she could feel the pull of his sexual attraction from the other side of his desk! His girlfriends would most likely fall head over heels in love with him.

But he wouldn't fall for them.

Oh, no! He would simply slake his physical hunger and keep his emotions intact. He would remain totally uninvolved. In that way, he wouldn't feel he was betraying his beloved Catherine and—

The door burst open and Staff Nurse Rona Phillips hurried inside. 'Sorry to interrupt you, sir, but one of our patients is haemorrhaging on the examination couch in Dr Hannah's room and—'

'Let's go!'

As Tessa followed Max, all her turbulent thoughts vanished, or rather shelved themselves in her subconscious from where they would resurface to taunt her as soon as she'd dealt with the emergency.

'Thanks for coming so quickly,' Hannah said, looking up briefly as she withdrew some blood from her patient's arm into a syringe.

Turning aside to place the blood sample in a sterile container, she briefly and quietly outlined the case.

'I'm taking some blood for grouping and cross-matching to determine Helen's blood group so that we can set up an intravenous drip to replace the blood that's been lost.'

It transpired that their patient, Helen Cooper, aged thirty-seven, had been losing small amounts of blood for a few days but had waited until she was due for her routine examination in Outpatients before she'd mentioned it to anyone.

'I hoped the bleeding might stop on its own,' their patient said in a weak voice as they gathered around the examination couch. 'I've been so fit all the way through the first seven months, I thought there couldn't be anything wrong with me. Is it something serious?'

'When you had your scan just now, we found that the placenta—that's the tube that takes nourishment from you to your baby—is leaking a little bit, Helen,' Hannah said gently.

'So we'd like you to come and stay on my ward so that we can look after you,' Tessa said quickly, noting the worried look on their patient's face. 'We'll phone your family so that they can make arrangements to cope without you for a while.'

'There's only my husband, Graham, at home. I'm not sure if he can manage without me,' Helen Cooper said doubtfully.

She leaned back wearily against the pillow. 'But I'd better do what you say. It's my first baby and very precious. I don't want to lose this one…like I did the last.'

The patient's voice faltered as she finished the sentence and Tessa looked down at the case notes to see if she could make sense of her words. If it was Helen Cooper's first baby, why was she referring to her last baby?

'I had a little girl when I was fifteen,' the patient continued in a dead voice.

'My mum persuaded me to have her adopted when she was just six weeks old. That was twenty-two years ago, but I can still see her pretty little face. She…'

Tessa took hold of Helen's hand as she watched her trying to hold back the tears.

'She was a lovely little thing. I wanted to keep her. I didn't want… I…'

Tessa spoke soothing words of comfort and, as she waited for the tears to subside, she looked across at Max. His eyes were troubled. They both knew this was going to be a difficult case with so much at stake.

Anne Reeves arrived to escort their patient to Nightingale. Tessa outlined the case to her staff nurse and asked that Helen be treated with more than usual tender loving care.

'We've got to save this baby,' she said quietly to Max

and Hannah, as the porter wheeled their patient out through the door.

'We'll do all we can,' Max said, in a studiously professional voice.

'But the scan showed that we've got a case of placenta praevia on our hands. Helen's placenta is too low down where it joins with the womb. Now that the womb is getting big, the stretching process causes the placenta to pull away. This is cutting off the baby's source of nourishment and causing the mother to bleed.'

Tessa didn't need to be told how grave the situation was. 'I've nursed cases of placenta praevia before, Max,' she said quietly. 'We'll give Helen a blood transfusion as soon as her blood group has been established. She'll have to stay in bed until her thirty-eighth week...unless she miscarries or the baby—' She broke off, not wanting to voice her fear that the unborn baby might die in the womb from lack of nourishment.

'I'm going back to Nightingale,' she said, affecting a brisk professionalism she didn't feel to cover up her concern. 'The main point to remember with this case is that we've got a very vulnerable mother who's pinning all her hopes on a replacement for the baby that was taken from her when she was barely out of childhood herself.'

Max put a hand on her shoulder.

'Don't get too emotionally involved, Tessa,' he said softly. 'You mustn't take on the problems of all your patients. We're professionals, remember, and we have to be able to put our emotions on one side.'

'Well, you'd know all about that, wouldn't you?' she said, under her breath, as she made for the door.

'What did you say? I couldn't hear what you said just then.'

She turned at the door and saw the perplexed expression on his face.

Hannah, who was tidying away the instruments on the examination trolley, clanking them into a pile ready for sterilisation, appeared oblivious to all around her.

'I said…'

She paused as she decided she'd done enough stirring up for the time being. She wasn't going to give up on unearthing Max's true emotions but she'd have to be more subtle.

'It wasn't important,' she said quietly.

His eyes flickered. 'I'll come up to Nightingale when I've finished my clinic. I'd like to do another examination on Helen. Don't get me wrong. I do agree with you that she should have priority treatment.'

'I'll see to it,' Tessa said evenly.

As she closed the door she wondered if she'd actually achieved something where Max was concerned. Was she beginning to get through to him, prising him out of that sterile vacuum he'd built around himself?

On the ward, she found Phil Dixon setting up the drip on her new patient.

'Everything OK, Phil?'

'Yes, Sister.'

He didn't even glance in her direction as he continued with his task.

Their house surgeon was a man of few words. But Tessa rated him as one of the most promising young doctors she'd come across during the whole of her nursing career so she had absolute confidence in him.

She sat down in the chair beside her bed. 'How are you feeling now, Helen?'

'I'm a bit worried about my husband, Graham, Sister. He can't boil an egg.'

'Then it's time he learned! You've got to concentrate on

looking after yourself. Has Graham got a mother or a sister who could—?'

'Oh, yes!'

Helen ran a hand through her greying hair.

'His mother would be over the moon to have him back on the farm for a while. You see. he was a bachelor, over forty and still living at home, until we married last year.'

She pulled a wry face. 'I don't think his mother was entirely happy to see him go and, to be honest, I've tried to keep him all to myself since we married. It's not that I'm jealous but…'

'You like to be self sufficient, don't you?' Tessa prompted.

Her patient smiled. 'That's it! You see, I'm a bit long in the tooth to be marrying and starting a family so—'

'You're only thirty-seven, Helen.'

'Well, I never thought it would happen to me. After I gave up my little girl for adoption I sort of put all my emotions on ice. Know what I mean, Sister?'

She certainly did! And, looking up at Max as he came in through the curtains of the cubicle, she knew that he, an expert at controlling his emotions, did too!

His eyes held a veiled expression as he looked down at her, sitting beside her patient. She didn't stand up. Some professionals might not approve of her easygoing relationship with her patients. She hoped Max wasn't one of those. If he was…tough! She still didn't intend to change her methods.

She wanted her patients to feel that they could unburden themselves upon her whenever they needed to. It was all part of the healing process. She was convinced that wounds healed quicker when people were content and happy.

Looking at Max now, his face an enigmatic mask, she wondered how long it would be before his deep emotional wound started to heal. That particular wound wouldn't heal until the patient wanted it to. And, from what she'd seen so far, Max was content to let his wound stay there for ever!

But why had it become so important to her that she turn him back into the man he used to be? And was it possible?

He was talking now to Phil Dixon, discussing how much intravenous blood their patient was going to need.

'I'll take over here, Phil,' Max said quietly. 'There are two new patients in the beds at the far end of the ward who need their case histories taken. I'd like you to go and see them.'

He smiled down at Helen as he gave her all his attention. With help from Tessa, he carried out a full examination of their patient. When he'd finished he explained that bed rest was going to be the most important part of the treatment.

'If you're lying still, the tube carrying nourishment to the baby has a better chance of doing its job, Helen,' he told his patient. 'I know it's boring but we'll try to find ways of keeping you occupied. Do you like reading?'

Helen nodded. 'I'll get Graham to bring some books in. And I'll keep very still if that's good for my baby.'

Max patted her hand. 'I can tell you're going to be a model patient.'

Tessa watched the happy smile spread across Helen's face. She noticed the grey hairs on her patient's head. Thirty-seven wasn't old, but it wasn't young either to be coping with a difficult pregnancy. It was a good thing her patient seemed to have a tough spirit. She was definitely a survivor.

'I'd like a word, Sister.'

Max's professional voice broke into her thoughts. She stood up, smoothing down the stiff cotton of her dark blue uniform dress.

'Of course, Mr Forster. Would you like to come into my office?'

They walked side by side down the ward. Closing the office door, she invited Max to sit down.

'I'll make some tea.' She took the kettle over to the sink and turned on the tap. 'I presume you want to discuss the new patients.'

'Not entirely.'

She plugged in the kettle before she turned round to look at him. He was sitting in one of the ancient but comfortable squashy chairs, one leg loosely draped over the small coffee-table. He looked relaxed. She found herself wondering what it would be like to spend some time with him in an off-duty situation.

Concentrate, girl! 'So, what else is on the agenda?' she said lightly, as she perched on the edge of her desk.

'I suppose you could call it a social obligation,' he began hesitantly.

Definitely intrigued now, she waited for him to elaborate, but he was in no hurry. It was as if he was searching for the right words. She felt her curiosity growing by the second.

'It's Francesca,' he said eventually.

'Francesca?'

'Yes. She's got it into her head she'd like to see you again, Tessa. Understandable, of course, because the two of you got on so well at Hannah and Simon's the other evening. And she's been asking me about the times when you used to babysit for her.'

He paused, his eyes searching her face. Running a hand through his dark hair in a gesture of semi-desperation, he carried on at breakneck speed, as if anxious now to get to the point. 'Now, I don't know anything about your off-duty life but could you find the time to come over for supper one evening?'

The kettle was boiling. She busied herself with pouring

the water into the teapot. Coming out of the blue, this invitation was something she was totally unprepared for.

'I'll have to check my off-duty,' she said quietly, willing herself to stay calm. 'I'm often on duty in the evenings.'

'Don't you organise your own duty roster on Nightingale, Sister?'

She swung round and saw that his lips had formed a teasing sort of smile. Was he making fun of her?

'Of course I do the roster! But I prefer to be on duty most evenings so that I'm here when the ward is handed over to the night staff.'

Turning her back, she resumed the teamaking. 'How do you take your tea?' she hurried on. 'Milk? Sugar?'

'A little milk, no sugar. Thank you.'

He took the cup from her hands.

'But all these evening duties—doesn't that play havoc with your social life?'

She lowered herself into the remaining squashy chair and took a sip of her tea, before smiling across the room at him.

'Are you trying to find out how much social life I have, Max? A clever try but my private life is strictly private.'

Strictly non-existent if the truth were known! But she didn't want to admit to Max that Nightingale had become the centre of her life. Keep him guessing!

She realised, with a pang, that she was flirting with him again. It wasn't that she fancied him...

Wasn't it? Why couldn't she admit to herself that she was beginning to find herself very much drawn towards him? She could cover up her feelings here in hospital but how would she cope if she went over to his house?

Only one way to find out. Take the plunge!

'I haven't done the duty roster for next week yet so I'll give myself an evening off. How about Wednesday?'

He pulled out a black leather diary from the inside pocket

of his jacket. There seemed to be an awful lot of engagements in there. She watched as he studied the scribbled entries.

'No, can't make Wednesday, sorry. Would Thursday be OK?'

She waited, before answering. It hadn't taken Max long to establish his social life here. She'd seen the way the unattached female staff had eyed him longingly. His evenings were probably fully booked for weeks ahead!

'Thursday will be fine,' she heard herself say.

He leaned back in his chair and smiled. 'Francesca will be so pleased.'

'I'm glad about that.'

The room seemed terribly quiet. Outside on the ward Tessa could hear the usual busy kind of noise. She put down her cup and stood up. Time to pick up the reins again.

'I'd better go and see the new admissions.'

'I'll come with you.'

They almost collided in the doorway. Max stood back, laughing. Looking up she saw that his often expressionless eyes were actually twinkling.

He bent down and put a hand on the back of her waist.

'After you, Sister.'

His hand on her waist was decidedly unnerving but she realised with a guilty pang that she was taking her time to go out into the corridor. On her own she would have moved much quicker than this!

CHAPTER THREE

TESSA slowed the car to a halt to avoid a straying sheep as she drove down the winding road into Cragdale. Waiting for it to make up its mind whether it was coming or going, she had time to look down into the valley towards the house where Max had lived when she'd first known him.

Ah, yes, there it was. Surrounded by a high, black, mill-stone grit wall, it looked like a fortress. She'd always felt safe there when she'd been babysitting. And the sound of the sheep on the hills and the cows in the surrounding fields hadn't disturbed her concentration as she'd churned out the required school essays, one ear cocked to listen for Francesca.

The little two-year old had always slept peacefully, apart from that one night when she'd been restless. That had been the night when Catherine Forster had taken her home.

She frowned as she remembered that two weeks ago at Hannah's supper party Max had said he'd been worried about Catherine driving because she hadn't been a very good driver. Now Tessa came to think about it, her driving had been rather erratic. She'd been glad to get back home all in one piece!

For a few, fleeting seconds she wondered if Catherine had been killed in a car crash. There had been a tragic accident, Simon Delaware had told her. Maybe…

She shivered as she made an effort to banish the awful thought from her mind and concentrate on the good times she'd known at the Forster house.

It had been such a happy house! How on earth Max could

bear to come back to Cragdale, with all the memories the valley held for him, she couldn't imagine.

Oh good, the sheep was moving now, scrambling over the wall back into the field.

'Don't break your leg,' she whispered as she watched its shambling progress.

But for all its clumsy movements the sheep was amazingly sure footed! It disappeared over the other side of the wall and Tessa breathed a sigh of relief as she let in the clutch and put her foot down gently on the accelerator.

Over in Riversdale, the valley that lay parallel to this one, her mother would be preparing supper. Since her father died ten years ago, Richard, her brother, and his wife had lived on the farm. Richard had a busy teaching schedule at a college in Leeds but Gemma had now given up her teaching job to be a full-time mother, looking after five-year-old Felicity and four-year-old Michael.

Having the young family under her roof, it was a great comfort to her mother. Tessa always intended to go home more often but sometimes a couple of weeks would slip by and when she made the dutiful phone call there would be a definite air of restraint at the other end.

It occurred to her now, as she changed into a lower gear to cope with the steep descent, that she could have gone over there this evening if she hadn't promised Francesca she would go for supper.

It was Francesca she was going to see, wasn't it? If Max happened to be there…

Who was she kidding? If Max happened to be there! He'd better be or this new outfit she'd bought would have been a waste of money.

She slowed down as she saw the beginning of the line of oak trees which Max had said marked their boundary. Yes, there it was. Oak Cottage.

Some cottage! she thought as she drove in through the wide gateway. The stone house at the end of the drive was enormous! Must have at least five bedrooms.

It was best not to think about bedrooms! Quickly, she turned her eyes to the exterior of the house. The grounds surrounding the so-called cottage were pretty extensive, too. The lawn nearest to the house was liberally punctuated with groups of daffodils. Primroses peeped from underneath the tall oak trees that stood like sentries guarding the drive.

'Tessa!'

Francesca appeared at the top of the wide stone steps leading into the house. She was wearing jeans and a sweater, Tessa noticed, her blonde hair loose and flowing casually over her shoulders.

Her first thought was that she, herself, was overdressed. But she comforted herself with the thought that Francesca was a young girl whereas she was a supposedly mature woman, even if she didn't feel like one at that precise moment.

She felt like a young, vulnerable teenager. Strange that she'd never felt like this when she'd breezed into the Forster household as a teenage babysitter!

Max had now appeared, also wearing jeans. Quite old, much-washed ones they looked from where she was standing, making an effort to lock the car door with fingers that refused to obey her.

'How charming you look, Tessa! It's good to see you out of uniform for a change.'

He was striding over towards her with an effortless panther-like movement. Was he being sarcastic? Did he think she was mad to wear this expensive suit to a midweek supper, which would probably be served in the kitchen?

At least it looked as if he intended to stay in and not leave her alone with Francesca. He surely wouldn't be going anywhere in old jeans and a denim shirt open at the neck, revealing far too much tanned skin and wayward dark hairs for her pulse rate to cope with!

Francesca was bounding along behind her father. She was a tall girl but even so she was having difficulty in trying to keep up with his long legs.

'Wow, what a fantastic suit! I love the colour. Sort of creamy, isn't it? Is it silk?'

Tessa told Francesca that her suit was, indeed, silk, all the while keeping her eyes warily on Max who was standing back with an amused smile on his face.

Francesca looked up at her father. 'I've never had anything made of silk.'

'Yes, you have. Your christening robe was white. Your mother made it from the train of her wedding dress.'

'Did she? I never knew that. Come on, let's go inside, Tessa. Would you like me to show you round the house? I love it here. It's got—'

'I think Tessa would probably like a drink after her long day at the hospital, Francesca,' Max said, as they all went up the steps.

'I'd love to see the house first,' Tessa said, avid with curiosity about the interior.

'OK, I'll have the drinks waiting when you've finished.'

Francesca was thorough in her whistle-stop tour of the house. As Tessa followed the exuberant girl from one beautifully furnished room to the next she was rapidly getting an impression of understated opulence. Precious antiques mingled with obviously treasured mementos of lesser value.

The oak-panelled dining room was dominated by a huge, carved oak table, surrounded by ten matching chairs. As Tessa had suspected, the dining room table wasn't set for supper. It was only when they went into the low-ceilinged, stone-flagged kitchen, warmed by an Aga, that she saw the setting for their meal. Cane placemats had been arranged on the long, old, scrubbed wooden table.

Max was standing by the Aga, a soup ladle in his hand.

'What do you think, Tessa?' he asked, in the professional voice he used when they were discussing a patient.

'Do you think there's too much garlic in this carrot soup? It's got coriander in as well, but I thought just a hint of garlic might be a good idea. I do like to experiment with the cooking.'

He was holding the large, antique, porcelain spoon towards her lips.

'I'm no expert,' she began, as the spoon was advanced to such a position that she had to open her mouth. 'Mmm... Yes, that's good. I like it.'

'And the garlic?'

'Didn't notice it.'

He raised one eyebrow. 'Perhaps a touch more garlic, then? It helps to keep away the vampires.'

Tessa laughed, relief flooding through her that Max still had his sense of humour.

Francesca put a hand on her arm. 'We haven't finished the tour yet. You haven't seen the bedrooms.'

'I think Tessa's seen enough, Francesca. The bedrooms can wait until after supper.'

He gave her a rakish grin. 'Oh dear, what an unfortunate turn of phrase. What I meant was—'

'I'd love to see the bedrooms now, Francesca,' Tessa said quickly.

The sooner she escaped from the kitchen, before Max saw the colour rising in her cheeks, the better!

The top floor of the house had two guest bedrooms with *en suite* bathrooms, one in lime green and the other, a very pretty, frilly, feminine sort of room, in pink. All totally refurbished and obviously unused, she noticed.

'This is my room,' Francesca said, flinging open a door on the first landing.

'It's a bit of a pigsty but Mrs Dewhirst comes in to clean on Mondays so I only have to clear up on Sunday nights.'

In spite of the teenage mess of discarded clothes, books and magazines, Tessa could see it was a delightful room.

'Lovely view of the garden,' she said, going over to the window.

'There's a much better view from Dad's room down the landing.'

Tessa was whisked out through the door.

'That's Dad's dressing room but it's full of boring men's clothes so we won't go in there. And this is his bedroom.'

Francesca was hurrying over to the window. 'There, what did I tell you about the view?'

It was, indeed, a beautiful and extensive view of the surrounding countryside. But it was the interior view of the bedroom that most intrigued Tessa! The vast four-poster bed. Was this where Max entertained his concubines?

'So, what do you think?'

She turned at the sound of his deep voice. He was leaning against the open door, a tantalising, almost seductive smile playing on his lips. She swallowed hard.

'About what?'

'The house. Do you like it? Do you think I made a good choice? I mean, would you have chosen a house like this?'

She gave a relieved laugh. 'If I could afford it. But I'm going to make do with that little cottage down there. Riverside Cottage. Look, you can just see it through the trees.'

As she pointed through the window she was very much aware that Max was standing behind her, far too close for comfort.

He put a hand on her shoulder. 'So we're going to be

neighbours. That's nice. I'll be able to pop down for a cup of sugar.'

'Could be a while yet. I'm still caught up in the house chain. The people who intend moving out of Riverside Cottage can't get into the house they're buying until the people who're supposed to be moving out of that one…you know, the usual hassle that goes on.'

Max moved round to lean against the window-sill. 'Buying a house can be a nerve-racking business. That's one of the reasons I'm renting this place.'

'What are the other reasons?' she surprised herself by saying, as curiosity got the better of her.

His eyes flickered. 'I don't want to put down roots here if…if it doesn't work out. I've taken the house for a year, with the option to buy at the end of it. The people who own it are working in the Far East.'

'But what about your work at Moortown General? Would you give that up after a year?'

'If I had to,' he said quietly. 'Nothing in life is ever permanent. Just when you think you've got it made, something comes along and— What I'm trying to say is that you have to be ready to move on.'

'Well, I like it here, Daddy,' Francesca said. 'I've made loads of friends already at Moortown School. And it's nice here in Cragdale. I'm glad we came back to the place where I was born.'

'I'm glad you're happy here. Now, let's go down and have some supper,' Max said quickly, leading the way out of his room.

Tessa sneaked a backward glance at the four-poster bed, wondering once more if Max had brought anyone from among the host of adoring females at the hospital to this sumptuous bedroom.

Banishing the unwelcome thought, she hurried back along the landing.

Max poured her a glass of wine in the kitchen as they sat around the kitchen table.

Francesca brought the soup tureen to the table, setting it down on a thick cork mat.

'I'm starving! Can we start supper, Dad?'

'Of course. You can serve.'

Francesca carefully ladled out the soup into warmed, willow-pattern soup bowls.

'This is delicious!' Tessa said. 'When did you learn to cook, Max?'

He smiled. 'I've always cooked. My parents were teachers. If I got home from school first I used to feed the hens, gather up the eggs and make myself an omelette. Would you like some bread, Tessa?'

She watched him carving a slice from the granary loaf in the middle of the table.

'You did that with the precision of a true surgeon,' she joked, as he placed the bread on her plate. 'Where did you live when you were a child?'

'We lived in a small cottage in Northumberland. Mum and Dad used to be worn out when they got in from school and they still had marking to do in the evening. It was a case of learn to cook or starve.'

Tessa saw the far-away expression in his eyes that she'd noticed so often. 'Were you an only child?'

He nodded. 'I don't think my parents could have coped with their professional lives and more than one child. They were very busy people. When they retired they sold up and bought a little house in the Greek islands so they could relax and do nothing but bask in the sunshine. That was always the dream they used to talk about.'

'When are you going to take me out to see my grand-parents, Dad?' Francesca said.

'When I can find the time.' Max was standing up, moving over to prepare the next course.

'I don't remember my grandparents at all,' Francesca told Tessa.

'They saw you when you were a baby,' Max said, as he lifted a roast chicken that was resting on the top of the Aga. 'Before they went out to Greece.'

He heaved the large dish onto the table and wiped his hands on a kitchen cloth.

'They're not typical grandparents, Francesca,' he said carefully. 'They weren't typical parents. They're very self-sufficient, content to be a couple on their own.'

He began carving slices from the chicken, again with the precision of the experienced surgeon. Tessa felt a surge of sympathy as she watched him.

He'd had to become self-sufficient from an early age. And it didn't seem as if he'd had much real love in his life—apart from his wife. If Catherine had been his only experience of real love, he must have been devastated when she died.

Francesca, too, seemed starved of the normal affection that exists in extended families.

'Are you in touch with relatives from your mother's family, Francesca?' she asked gently.

Francesca screwed up her face in concentration. 'I think there's an old aunt still alive somewhere but I've never met her. My mother's parents died when she was still at school, I think. Am I right, Dad?'

'Yes,' Max said quietly. 'Catherine's parents were middle-aged when she was born. I think they'd accepted the fact that they were childless and then, unexpectedly, along came Catherine.'

Tessa felt another pang of sympathy as she heard the special tone of voice that Max used when he spoke Catherine's name.

There was fresh fruit and cheese to follow the chicken. Tessa ate a couple of green, seedless grapes as she cut a small portion of Camembert from the cheese platter in the middle of the table.

'Coffee, Tessa?'

'Yes, please.' She watched Max spooning ground coffee into the cafetière.

'I'll have to get on with my homework, Dad.' Francesca was pulling a wry face as she stood up. 'Thanks ever so much for coming over, Tessa. You will come again, won't you?'

Tessa glanced at Max, but his back was towards her as he poured boiling water on to the coffee grounds.

'Yes, I'd love to,' she said quickly.

No response from Max. What would his reaction be? It was such a difficult situation. She didn't want to impose herself on him but...

He was turning round now but his bland expression gave her no indication of how he was feeling.

'Will you come up and say goodbye before you go, Tessa?' Francesca asked.

'Yes, of course.'

The kitchen door closed. They were alone. Now she really did feel it would be nice to know what Max was thinking!

He poured her a cup of coffee in a small, willow-pattern cup.

'Let's take our coffee into the sitting room,' he said, scraping back his chair on the stone-flagged floor.

'What about the washing up?' She was ever the practical one.

'Oh, I'll stick it all in the dishwasher after you've gone.'

Ah, so he wasn't planning to invite her to be one of his concubines! she thought, as she followed him along the corridor to the sitting room.

He removed a wrought-iron fireguard to reveal a cheery blaze of logs.

'I lit this when I came in,' he said, as he tossed another log on the fire. 'The central heating is perfectly adequate but I always think a fire is so welcoming, don't you?'

She agreed as she sat down on the cretonne-covered sofa. He joined her at the other end. A companionable silence descended—at least Tessa hoped it was companionable. Maybe Max would prefer to be on his own. She took another sip of coffee from the delicate cup.

'You've got some lovely crockery,' she remarked in a bright, conversational tone.

He smiled. 'Oh, it's all courtesy of the house. I'm renting the whole caboodle, lock stock and barrel. I sold everything we had over in the States. It didn't seem worth shipping it all over.'

'Wasn't that a wrench? I mean, didn't some of it have sentimental value?'

He gave a harsh laugh. 'Sentimentality is a luxury I can live without. It only gets in the way.'

'In the way of what?'

He shrugged. 'Life, the business of earning a living. Going from day to day without too much pain.'

She drew in her breath. 'That sounds like existence, not life.'

'It's called survival.'

End of conversation! There wasn't much she could add to that line of talk. She tried again.

'The rent for this place must be exorbitant,' she said, glancing around at the opulent furnishings and delicate antiques.

'Not really. The people were more interested in securing a good tenant who would take care of their house, so they let me have it for a peppercorn rent. I knew the sort of price I could afford to pay from the money I invested after I'd sold up in the States and they agreed on what I offered them.'

She put down her cup and saucer on the coffee-table in front of the sofa. 'A convenient arrangement.'

A log fell out of the fire onto the hearth. Max leapt to his feet and picked up the fire tongs to put it back on the red embers. He was allowing the fire to die down, she noticed. Time to go!

She stood up. 'I've got to be getting back,' she said.

He turned round, still holding the fire tongs. She noticed he'd wiped a hand over his face, and had left a dirty smudge on his cheek.

She smiled as she moved towards him. 'You look like the chimney sweep in the story of *The Water Babies*. Hold still, I've got a tissue in my bag.'

She reached up to dab at the streaky soot.

'There. That's better.' She made to move her hand but he caught hold of her wrist.

'Thanks, Tessa.' His voice was husky.

And then he kissed her, oh, so gently on the cheek. She looked up into his eyes as he pulled away again and was surprised to see real tenderness.

She tried to convince herself that it was only a friendly kiss. They were old friends, remember? And when old friends kissed there was nothing significant about it.

Then why was her heart thumping madly? Why did her legs feel like jelly? Why did she wish he would take her in his arms and—?

'I promised to say goodnight to Francesca,' she said quickly, as she turned and made for the door.

Running up the stairs with winged feet, she wished he would run after her and sweep her into his arms. She knew she was being irrationally romantic. Impossibly romantic, if she faced the facts. There was no way that Max was ever going to shake off the binding spell that Catherine held over him.

And she didn't want anything else—even if he were to offer it, which seemed unlikely. She didn't want to be on hand to help assuage his physical needs. Sex without love made no sense to her.

Walking along the landing towards Francesca's room she remembered the couple of real affairs she'd had during the past ten years—interesting enough for a short while, but she'd been glad to end them when the initial spark had died.

She knew she hadn't been in love with either Danny or Ben. For the past couple of years she'd been holding off, chasing some romantic idea that she was saving herself for the man of her dreams.

She tapped lightly on Francesca's door.

'How's the work going?' she asked when Francesca showed her inside.

Francesca grimaced. 'I'm trying to cram for a biology test tomorrow.'

Tessa smiled as she glanced down at the book on Francesca's desk.

'The digestive system. All those dear little enzymes busying themselves digesting the food we pour down the chute. I always think it's amazing how they can sort it all out without tripping over each other.'

Francesca laughed. 'Have you time to test me, Tessa? Just this page,' she wheedled.

Tessa picked up the book and sat down on the edge of Francesca's bed. 'Just this page and then I really must go.'

After a few minutes, during which she'd become impressed by Francesca's grasp of the subject, she stood up.

'You know, you really don't need to worry. I think the best thing you could do now is to get a good night's sleep.'

Francesca smiled. 'OK. If that's what you prescribe. Thanks, Tessa. It's so nice to have a woman who cares in the house. When Dad used to bring one of his girlfriends home I felt as if I was in the way...but with you it's different.'

'That's probably because I knew you when you were little,' she said quickly.

'Not entirely,' Francesca said quietly. 'No, you're different. I was glad when he told me he'd invited you for supper.'

Aha! So it hadn't been Francesca's idea. It was Max who'd invited her!

'Actually, you're the first person he's invited round since we moved here.'

Why did she feel a sense of relief?

'I suppose your dad had lots of girlfriends in the States,' Tessa said lightly.

'Not really. There were only two that I can remember. There hasn't been anyone for ages. I—'

She broke off, her eyes straying to the half-open door where Max was standing, his hand on the doorknob, an enigmatic smile playing on his lips.

'Giving away all my wicked secrets, Francesca?' he said in a teasing voice.

'Oh Dad, there was nothing wicked about Carol and...what was the other woman called?'

'Vanessa,' Max said.

'Yes, Vanessa. The boring one. I couldn't stand her and I'm sure the feeling was mutual because—'

'Have you finished your homework, Francesca?' Max was frowning now, trying to play the stern father.

'Yes, Tessa tested me and I passed, didn't I? Let's hope I can remember it all in the morning.'

'I must be off,' Tessa said quickly. 'Goodnight, Francesca.'

It seemed perfectly natural to drop a kiss on the young girl's cheek. For a moment Francesca held on to her.

'Come again soon, Tessa.'

'I will,' she said, studiously avoiding Max's eyes.

She followed him down the stairs to the front door where he turned and stood, looking down at her.

'Do I get a kiss too?' he said, still in the same teasing tone he'd used with Francesca.

Keep it light, she told herself. Don't spoil it.

Smiling up at him, she said, 'You had a kiss already.'

'That wasn't a kiss,' he said huskily. 'That was an exploratory operation to see how the patient would react.'

She felt a shiver of excitement running down her spine. Got to keep calm! She could feel the tension rising between them.

'And how did the patient react, Doctor?'

'Very favourably,' he said. 'She wasn't frightened of the situation at all.'

And then he took her in his arms. Slowly, oh, so slowly, he brought his lips down on hers. She felt limp with liquid desire and as he pulled her against him she gave up on all thoughts except one. If he asked her to stay the night she would find it very difficult to resist the temptation!

But he was already pulling himself away, running a hand down the side of her cheek before putting his hand out towards the doorknob.

He gave her a rakish grin. 'I'd better let you go before I shock you with a wild suggestion.'

'I'm sure I don't know what you mean,' she said, continuing with a psuedo make-believe coyness.

She ducked under his arm and prised open the door. The fresh air flooded in, reviving her sanity. She told herself she was glad he'd stopped when he did. Even though she prided herself on having brilliant self-control in most situations, an affair of the heart was quite different.

He followed her out to the car, holding open the driver's door until she was safely ensconced on her seat. The security lights had come on, bathing her in a bright, revealing glow when she would have preferred darkness to hide the turbulent emotions that must surely be showing on her face.

'Goodnight, Max. Thanks for the excellent supper.'

As she drove away she could see in her rear-view mirror that he was still standing in the drive.

CHAPTER FOUR

TESSA couldn't believe that Max's attitude towards her in hospital was still the same! Although he'd invited her out to his house for supper, nothing had changed. Apparently, the fact that he'd held her in his arms in a decidedly warm embrace meant nothing to him. But it did reinforce her theory that he was incapable of real emotion.

Furiously, she scribbled her signature on the report in front of her and closed the file. Looking up at the clock on the wall of her office, she realised she'd have to check on the new admissions. This wasn't the time to start worrying about Max's cool, clinical attitude towards her during the last week.

But once again she found herself frustrated by the fact that she couldn't get through to him. True, she'd only seen him on the ward, but he might have given her some indication that they were, at least, good friends.

Talk of the devil! As Max poked his head round the door, she wondered what he would say if she told him she was finding it difficult to stop thinking about him. Probably run a mile!

'Coffee?'

That was, after all, no more than she would offer to any of the other medical personnel who called in mid-morning.

'Thanks.'

He came in and slid into a chair.

She thought he was looking tired as she noted the vague dark patches under the eyes. Submerging her natural instinct for caring, she refrained from remarking on the fact as she poured out a cup from the cafetière.

'So, is this a social call or…?'

'I've come to see Jill Mason, our surrogate mother of twins. Has she been admitted yet?'

His tone was ultra professional. She knew she hadn't imagined the coolness of his attitude during the past week. Perhaps he was regretting the warmth of his goodnight kiss. Warmth! That kiss had been positively scorching and far too disturbing.

She put a hand to her lips where his sensual mouth had tantalised her. Had it been a dream?

Oh, no! The reality was sitting right there in front of her. But it might as well have been a dream for all the effect it seemed to have had on Max.

She picked up her stiff cuffs from the desk and shot them over the navy blue sleeves of her uniform dress.

'Staff Nurse Reeves is helping Jill unpack and settling her into bed.'

Was her voice professional enough? She cleared her throat.

'I've put her next to Josie Hargreaves, our triplets mother-to-be. I think they might get on well together.'

'Good idea! They've both got to be patient while they wait. It will be a few weeks before we can deliver their babies so they can keep each other company.'

'If they can chat to each other when they're feeling bored the time will pass much quicker,' she said, pleased that he was showing his approval. 'It makes my job much easier if the patients stay happy. It's when they start worrying inwardly about imaginary problems that—'

'Yes, but you must remember that you're here primarily to help their physical needs, not to worry about their psychological state of mind, Tessa.'

'In my experience, you can't separate the two,' she countered in an even tone. 'A healthy mind makes for a healthy body.'

His brown eyes flickered. 'Not entirely. Sometimes you can have a healthy body even though the mind can be in turmoil.'

'Are you speaking from your own experience?' she asked quietly.

He hesitated. 'Yes. I've been to hell and back but it didn't affect my health and strength. I was still able to function in every area of my life.'

She put down her cup and stood up. '"Function" being the operative word.'

Her hand was on the doorknob but he crossed the room and restrained her from turning it.

'What did you mean by that?'

He was standing very close to her, looking down at her with flashing eyes.

Good! She'd annoyed him. She'd shaken him out of his apathy. Anything was better than the bland exterior he'd presented during the past week. She would fire up his sluggish emotions if it was the last thing she did!

'I was talking about the chemistry between people. The tension that makes the sparks fly. Life would be very boring if there was no animated interaction between people.'

A slow smile spread across his lips. It was the first time she'd seen him smile in days and she breathed an inward sigh of relief.

'Is that the end of the psychology lecture, Sister? Can we go and see the patients now?'

She noticed that his voice was perfectly calm but she knew she'd ruffled his feathers!

She nodded. Already he was looking more animated, more like the human being she'd glimpsed when they'd had supper together. His emotions were still intact. They just needed a kick-start to get them going. He could function on a physical level—oh, yes, no problem there! But real, honest-to-goodness, warm relationships seemed beyond him.

Given time, she intended to change that!

As they walked down the ward together, she heard Helen Cooper calling out to her.

'I'll come over to see you, Helen,' she said quickly.

Poor Helen! Tessa never kept her waiting if she could help it. Their patient with the badly placed placenta was constantly worrying about the outcome of her pregnancy. Every time Tessa went near her she was inundated with questions.

Max followed her over to Helen's bed. Tessa noticed that Helen's grey-streaked auburn hair was looking greasy and losing its shape since being on the ward and she made a mental note to mention it to the hospital hairdresser. A cut and blow-dry might help Helen's morale.

'I've been bleeding again this morning, Sister, you know, down below. Not much, but enough to make me worried again.'

Tessa pulled the curtains round the bed.

'We'll have a look at you, Helen, and see what we can do.' She looked up at Max. 'Shall I bring the examination trolley, sir?'

'Yes, please, Sister.'

He leaned over to chat to Helen and Tessa was pleased to see the way he could elicit information from his patients while making it seem as if they were having a conversation. Yes, he certainly had a good bedside manner.

When she returned with the trolley they were still engrossed in animated conversation. Max had gained Helen's confidence and from there it was easy to perform a full examination on the relaxed patient.

He straightened up at the end of his examination and smiled reassuringly at Helen.

'Nothing to worry about. As I told you when you came in, the tube delivering nourishment to your baby is slightly misplaced. That's why you've experienced the bleeding. But the baby's heart beat is strong. All the indications are that he's a healthy baby so—'

'Why did you say he? I'd hoped it would be a little girl like my lovely Susan.'

As Tessa watched the deep frown form on her patient's face she reached down and took hold of her hand.

'I've no idea of the sex of your baby,' Max said quickly. 'I wasn't there when you had your last scan and in your notes it says you've requested that we don't tell you. So, of course, that piece of information hasn't been recorded.'

Helen nodded gravely. 'I don't want to know because I want it to be like when Susan was born twenty-two years ago—a complete surprise. Nobody told me she was going to be a girl.'

She gave a little sniff. 'I was trying not to bond with her because I knew I'd have to give her up for adoption when she was six weeks old and...'

Tessa squeezed her patient's hand and pulled a tissue out of the box on the bedside locker.

'Now, don't upset yourself again, Helen. Soon you'll have another little baby and—'

'I'll call her Susan if she's a girl,' Helen said, wiping away her tears. 'I really do hope it's another girl.'

Tessa didn't reply as she hugged the secret deep inside her. She'd been at Helen's last scan and from the blurred images she'd seen on the screen she was ninety-nine per cent sure it was a girl. She only hoped it was going to survive the last critical weeks.

She outlined her fears for the baby's safety to Max in a quiet voice as soon as they left their patient.

He nodded. 'We'll deliver the baby as soon as he reaches a viable size.'

'I think it's a girl,' Tessa said. 'I've seen the scan.'

'Helen will be thrilled.'

'A replacement for Susan,' Tessa said quietly. 'I'm not sure if it's a good idea to replace people like that.'

'I don't think you can ever replace one individual with another,' Max said slowly.

He'd paused in the middle of the ward and was looking down at her, his eyes searching her face.

'I don't think you should even try,' she said, her eyes unblinking as she looked up at him. 'When a person has gone for ever you can't replace them. But that doesn't mean you have to spend your entire life wishing they were with you.'

She saw his lower lip tremble almost imperceptibly.

'Do you think that's what Helen has done?' he said evenly.

'From what she's told me, yes, I do. She's wasted twenty-two years longing for a child that was taken from her.'

'Probably not all wasted years,' he said quietly. 'People can function in a normal way even when they're eaten up with sorrow.'

' ''Function'' being the operative word,' she said.

He gave her a wry smile. 'That's the second time you've told me that this morning. Look, Tessa, I know what you're getting at and—'

'We'd better see to our patients,' she said quickly. 'They're beginning to wonder why we're standing here in the middle of the ward, having a decidedly controversial conversation.'

She moved quickly towards Jill Mason's bed. Their patient was sitting on the edge of her bed deep in conversation with her neighbour, Josie Hargreaves. As Tessa approached she heard Josie laughing about something that Jill had said.

Looking up at Max, she said, 'Jill and Josie seem to be getting on like a house on fire.'

'They're lucky to have a brilliant psychologist for a ward sister.'

She noticed that his eyes held an enigmatic expression.

'Pure common sense,' she said evenly, not knowing whether he'd meant the remark as a compliment.

Probably not! Probably he was getting fed up with her analytical approach. Tough! Because she didn't intend to change, especially where he was concerned. He needed his emotional problems sorted out just like her patients did.

Standing between the two beds, she smiled at Jill and Josie. 'So, how are you feeling today, ladies?'

Jill patted the mound beneath her white towelling dressing-gown. 'I'm sure someone put football boots on these two boys during the night.'

'You've only got two,' Josie called across good-naturedly. 'I've got three little ones to worry about.'

She looked suddenly very concerned. 'Mr Forster, do you think I could have a word with you this morning? It's nothing serious but…'

'Of course.'

As Tessa pulled the curtains round Josie's bed she saw that Jill was lying back against her pillows, covering her ears with her headphones.

How diplomatic of Jill to make it quite clear she wasn't going to listen to what Josie had to say.

Tessa joined Max beside Josie's bed.

'As you know, this is my last-ditch attempt at a family,' Josie was saying quietly. 'I'm forty-two and if this fails I'm not going to try again.'

'There's no reason to think you'll fail, Josie,' Tessa said, quickly. 'All the indications so far are very favourable.'

Josie grabbed a tissue and blew her nose vigorously.

'But I've had three miscarriages—two were babies I conceived naturally and then twins were put inside me after they'd survived whatever it is they do to make them grow in the test tubes. That last attempt was just like the three babies I've got inside me now.'

Josie screwed up her face anxiously. 'I was devastated when I lost those twins. I almost didn't try again. So I can't help thinking every time these triplets stop moving around inside me that...'

Tessa squeezed Josie's hand as she dabbed at her eyes with another tissue. She waited for her to finish voicing all her fears. It was important for the patient to get it off her chest.

'I like to appear bright and breezy. It's in my nature to be cheerful,' Josie continued. 'I pretend I'm not worrying but I can't help it.'

Max put a Pinard's stethoscope, the cone-shaped instrument for listening to the heartbeats of unborn babies, against Josie's abdomen. A few moments elapsed before he straightened up, his face calm and smiling.

'There's a lot of healthy activity in there and the babies' hearts are beating strongly. But just to reassure you we'll arrange for you to go down for another scan this morning. When you see your babies moving on the screen you'll feel reassured that all is well.'

'Now, you mustn't worry, Josie,' Tessa said. 'Your other pregnancies only lasted three months or less, didn't they? You're already more than six months so this pregnancy is well established. If you can rest and relax for the final weeks you'll have three healthy babies to take home with you.'

She smiled reassuringly at her patient. 'It's funny, you know, I didn't think you were the worrying kind.'

Josie put on a brave smile. 'I keep it all bottled up.'

'Well, don't keep it bottled up now you're in hospital,' Tessa said gently. 'Any time you've got a problem just call me over.'

'Sister likes sorting out other people's problems,' Max said evenly. 'You're very lucky to have been put on this ward.'

'Perhaps you'd rather I ignored my patients' cries for help, Max,' Tessa said quietly a few minutes later as they walked away from Josie's bedside.

'Not at all! I think your approach is admirable on the ward. I just think it's misplaced when you try to practise it on me. I don't need any help sorting out my life, thank you.'

They had reached her office. She turned at the door and faced him, her hand on the knob.

'Well, that's fine. If you're perfectly happy, then I won't interfere again.'

She turned to open the door but he put a hand on her arm. 'It's not that I'm not grateful, Tessa. It's just that…there's nothing you can do. I know from past experience that this is the only way I can cope with…what happened.'

'What did happen, Max?'

His veiled eyes flickered for an instant before he spoke. 'It's all in the past. I prefer not to resurrect it.'

'You're worse than Josie, keeping your problems all bottled up,' she said, with a brusqueness that probably seemed almost brutal, but which she hoped would be effective.

'A problem shared is a problem halved,' she went on relentlessly. 'Look, I'm off duty this afternoon. I know you haven't got a clinic so what do you say we go for a long walk and you can tell me what's eating you, Max?'

He ran a hand through his hair as he frowned down at her. 'You're a very forward young lady—you know that, don't you?'

She nodded apprehensively, feeling the thumping of her heart as she watched him. She might be forward but she was truly scared at that moment. He might be an old friend but he was also a consultant and her boss.

Suddenly his expression changed and he gave her a wry smile.

'OK, you're on...for the walk, that is. I could do with some fresh air. But I won't be talking about anything except the beautiful countryside. Those are my terms. Take it or leave it, Sister!'

She smiled. 'I'll take it.'

It shouldn't be difficult to worm something out of him during the course of their walk. She glanced out of the corridor window.

'It's a perfect spring day. Absolutely ideal. We could skip lunch and make an early start. I'll fix us a picnic. Let's say one o'clock in the car park, shall we?'

Strike while the iron is hot! She went into her room, leaving the door wide open, but he didn't follow her.

She'd half expected that he wouldn't turn up but there he was, waiting for her in his distinctive, steel grey BMW as she carried out the packets of food she'd just collected from the kitchen.

He hadn't seen her. She knocked on his window. It slid down with a whirring electrical sound.

'You're late.'

'Sorry, I had to wait in the kitchen for the lunch.'

He raised an eyebrow. 'OK, I'll forgive you. Hop in.'

He leaned across to open the passenger door. 'I thought it would be safer to take my car.'

'Why safer?' she asked, fastening her seat belt as she settled down into the depths of the ultra-comfortable leather seat.

Mmm, she'd always loved the feel and the smell of real leather!

He was driving out through the hospital gateway, acknowledging the military-style salute of the porter on duty in his little sentry-box. For a few seconds he didn't reply and she repeated her question.

'It's safer because I know I'm a good driver, whereas you…'

'Yes?' She waited.

'You're an unknown quantity. You might be a good driver. On the other hand—'

'On the other hand I'm a woman. Is that it?'

'Not at all.'

They'd pulled up at the traffic lights halfway down the high street outside the new boutique she meant to check out when she could find the time. Part of the window display was given over to lacy underwear. She'd never worn anything so exotic. Was it time to start now?

She had the sudden urge to become wildly feminine! Did Max like feminine women with frills and flounces or a girl like herself who'd barely had time to dab a streak of lipstick on after she'd changed into ancient jeans and a sweater?

She glanced in the vanity mirror. Mmm, she didn't look too bad considering the small amount of time she'd had to transform herself from Nightingale Sister.

'So you agree that women can drive as well as men?' she said, as the car moved slowly forward past the roadworks where they were digging large holes for some unknown purpose and up the hill towards the moorland road.

He was pulling a wry face. 'I didn't say that. I imagine,

because you're a very efficient type of person that you probably drive well, but some women are hopeless.'

'Like your wife, you mean?'

Oh, God, that was brutal, but she'd said it now!

'Why do you say that?' he asked evenly.

'When we were at Hannah's and Simon's you told me she wasn't a very good driver.'

'Did I say that? I don't usually talk about it.'

She gripped the edge of the leather seat. 'What is there to talk about, Max?'

'Nothing I want to discuss at the moment,' he said quickly. 'You'll have to direct me along this road, Tessa. It's ages since I was up here on the moors. Let's have the picnic first so that we don't have to carry all those packages around with us. Where do you suggest?'

'There's a small track about a mile further on—leads down to a little stream. That should be a picturesque place for our cheese sandwiches.'

He smiled. 'Is that what we've got?'

'I've no idea. The cook was busy when I phoned down from the ward this morning. One of the kitchen staff told me she'd do what she could but it was very short notice. Apparently, I should have made my request yesterday and put it in writing. But I didn't know I would be going on a picnic today, did I?'

She was watching the road carefully. 'Slow down, Max, we're nearly— Turn now!'

'This rough track is playing havoc with my tyres,' Max said after a few minutes as he negotiated another stony section.

'Sorry about that. We've had a few storms during the winter and the unmade tracks out here always get churned up. But it's worth it, don't you think? Just look at those bluebells over there!'

He was smiling now. 'I'll admire them when we get to the bottom of this track.'

He ground to a halt barely yards from a stream which had swollen to river-like proportions during the winter weeks of relentless rain. He produced a rug from the boot of the car and spread it on the grass.

Tessa unfolded two large paper napkins beside the stream and proceeded to unwrap the mystery parcels.

'Cheese and pickle, cheese and tomato…'

'Or just plain cheese, I expect,' Max said, leaning back against a large boulder.

He picked up a flat stone and sent it skimming across the stream. He smiled as it hit a boulder on the other side with a resounding thwack.

'Haven't done that since I was a kid.'

'I remember you told me you lived in Northumberland,' she said, delving further into the food packages. 'Beautiful countryside up there… Guess what? I've found some ham.'

'Yes, please.'

He held out his hand and she put a sandwich in the middle of his large palm.

'I was born and brought up in Northumberland,' he said, standing up as he bit into the thick, chunky sandwich. 'I'll get the wine.'

'Wine? That's nice. I was going to offer you one of these little plastic fruit juice packets but they don't look very exciting.'

'I picked up a bottle from my rooms. Walking is thirsty work.'

She munched on a cheese and pickle sandwich as she watched him uncorking the wine. The sound of the rushing stream in the background was very soothing. Already she could see a change in Max. He looked relaxed as he sat on the rug, pulling out the cork from the bottle and pouring wine into a couple of steel picnic cups.

'Cheers!' She raised the cup to her lips. 'We don't often get warm days like this in April.'

He was half turned towards her, propped up on one elbow. 'I remember how I enjoyed the first days of spring when I was a child. We lived very near the sea and I used to spend hours on the shore building castles, collecting pebbles and…generally messing about.'

'Were you always by yourself?'

There was a far-away expression in his eyes as he smiled. 'Yes. There were no children living nearby and my parents were too busy to come with me. I was always alone but I was never lonely.'

'I suppose that's where you learned to be self-sufficient,' she said quietly.

For an instant his enigmatic eyes locked with hers. 'Not entirely.'

He reached across and topped up her cup with wine.

'I think you learn to be self-sufficient as you go through life,' he said.

'So long as you don't build a wall around yourself and erect a keep out sign,' she said, trying to keep her tone light.

He put down the bottle on a flat stone and faced her. 'Is that what you think I do?'

'Well, don't you?'

He leaned back against the boulder. 'If I choose to. But I removed the sign long enough to have had a couple of relationships since Catherine died.'

This was more like it. He was beginning to open up. She held her breath.

'It was purely physical with both Vanessa and Carol. Oh, they both wanted to pursue it further but I felt nothing for them.'

'Did they know you were just using them?'

'I wasn't just using them!' He sat up. 'My God, you're the boldest, most unsubtle, most infuriating...'

He leaned across and grabbed hold of her by the shoulders. 'It's none of your business, Tessa. You keep trying to—'

He broke off. His hands were ruffling her hair as he looked into her eyes.

'Why do you have to be so persistent?' he whispered huskily. 'Just when I thought I'd got myself sorted out, you come along and upset everything I...'

His lips closed on hers and she heard his deep sigh mingling with her own. He pulled her against him and she could feel the beating of his heart against hers.

Gently, oh, so gently, he released her from his embrace, his eyes again searching her face as if trying to gain her reaction.

He gave her a rakish grin. 'Let's go for that walk. Otherwise we may stay here all afternoon.'

She could think of nothing she'd like better than an afternoon by the stream with Max! But their deal had been for a walk so she wouldn't change the agreement.

He put out a hand and pulled her to her feet. For a few moments they stood together. It was almost as if Max was struggling with his feelings, trying to decide how far to pursue this warm encounter. Suddenly he turned away.

Tessa bent down to pick up the debris of their picnic, putting everything into a large plastic bag. Max put the stopper in the wine bottle and gathered up the cups.

'We've only drunk half of it,' he said.

'Just as well. I wouldn't want you to have to carry me over the moors.'

He smiled. 'That wouldn't be a problem. I wouldn't think

you weigh very much. You look pretty skinny from where I'm standing.'

'Is that a compliment or…?'

'Take it how you like.'

He took two strides towards her, wrapping his arms gently around her. She dropped the plastic bag on the grass as his arms tightened.

His kiss was gentle. She closed her eyes to savour the moment. Because it was only a moment before he pulled away. She could hear his increased rate of breathing as he formed his next words.

'Let's go!'

He put out a hand and led her back to the car. They deposited their picnic debris in the boot. As he folded away the rug she gathered that he'd made his decision. They were definitely going for that walk.

Just as well, she thought as she followed Max up the steep woodland path that led to the moors. She knew she would have found it difficult to resist his advances. In the few moments she'd spent in his arms she'd discovered just how much she wanted to be with him.

But, as Max had discovered from obviously bitter experience, purely physical relationships were unsatisfactory. And she knew instinctively that she wouldn't be satisfied with a purely physical relationship. Exciting though it might be, it wouldn't be enough for her.

Not where Max was concerned. Watching him now, climbing up the steep path, she could see the strong muscles in his legs straining against the denim of his jeans. The layers of woollen sweaters that shrouded his upper body couldn't hide the fact that he was slim and well honed.

He obviously worked out or played tennis or some other sport to keep him in such good shape. She caught her breath. There was a deep physical need inside her which Max had stirred just now. Her sensual feelings had been dormant for so long she'd begun to think they'd died before they'd had time to flower!

What did she feel like? A woman... Dare she say it—a woman in love? No, it was pure fantasy. She couldn't be falling in love with this impossible man...could she? This impossible, highly desirable, extremely handsome...

He'd reached the top of the hill and was turning round, his face wreathed in smiles. 'Just look at the view!'

She increased her pace. He leaned down and held out his hand to haul her up the final rough section to the summit. As his fingers closed around hers she felt a deep rush of desire. Looking down into the valley, she saw the spot where he'd kissed her—twice! She could still feel the sensual tingling of her lips in her imagination.

He put an arm gently round her waist as he turned her to look in the other direction.

'See the whole panorama!' he said excitedly. 'The dark brown of the hills to the north and the softer rolling fields to the south. And the springy, heathery texture of the moors.'

She smiled. 'That's one thing we have in common, Max. I adore the countryside up here. The year is still young. I love it when the heather turns a vivid purple towards the end of the summer.'

'And the yellow gorse comes into full flower and... We'll have to come up here again later in the year.'

He released her hand and moved forward along the moorland path.

She followed behind. 'Ah, so you're intending to stay at Moortown till the end of the summer?' She kept her tone deliberately jocular.

'I might,' he called back, without looking round. 'If I

don't get too many badgering questions. I'm a free spirit. If I feel like taking off again, that's what I'll do.'

'I'm sure you will. Oh, look at that darling little lamb, Max.'

Near to the path a large, shaggy, winter-coated ewe was licking its newborn offspring. The tiny lamb stood on its spindly legs, shivering with the change of temperature from its mother's warm womb to the bleak northern moorland. It gave a weak cry, before nuzzling under its mother to find the source of nourishment.

'See how it latches on instinctively,' Tessa said. 'It's almost worth bringing some of my mothers and babies up here for a lesson in breast feeding.'

He laughed. 'Don't you dare! We'll keep this place a secret.'

He was looking down at her with a quizzical expression and she wondered exactly what he'd meant by his last remark. Did he mean it was their secret place, up here where she felt as if she was on top of the world?

He was turning round to continue the walk. Better not read too much into it.

'If we turn right where the path forks we could walk down into Riversdale,' she said after a few minutes. 'Mum would give us a cup of tea.'

She held her breath. This hadn't been on the agenda when she'd set off but she had the sudden urge to take Max to meet her mother. But wasn't this exactly the sort of situation that would frighten him off?

He hadn't replied. She knew she shouldn't have pushed her luck.

'Do you think your mother will have baked some of her oat cakes?' he asked, just when she'd given up hope of him even considering her impulsive suggestion.

Oh, she could have hugged him right there in the middle

of the path! But she didn't. Instead, she smiled to herself as she replied, as nonchalantly as she could, 'She might. We'll never know unless we trek down there, will we?'

'You're on.'

Tessa brushed the dust from her jeans as she reached the bottom of the Riversdale path. Ahead lay the short stretch of metalled road that led to her home.

She paused at the top of the cobbled drive leading down to Fold Farm. She could see Fred, the elderly man who was now the only full-time employee on the farm, scattering corn over the farmyard for the hens that clucked around his baggy trousered legs.

He waved the arm that wasn't holding the bucket. 'Well, if it isn't young Tessa. Your mother's been saying it was high time you paid us a visit.'

'Hello, Fred. How are you?'

'As well as can be expected, lass, considering me artheritis. Gets me something shocking it does when it rains. Who's your friend, Tessa?'

'This is Max Forster.'

'How d'you do, sir?' Fred touched the front of his cap. 'Kettle's on inside and t' missus 'as been baking so she'll see thee all right.'

'So, the wanderer returns!' Mrs Grainger said, as Tessa and Max walked in through the open kitchen door. 'I was beginning to think you'd gone back to London.'

Tessa walked across the large, high-ceilinged, stone-flagged kitchen and kissed her mother on the cheek. 'I've been so busy, Mum. Haven't had a minute.'

'I bet you haven't!' Mrs Grainger said, her eyes twinkling as she subjected the handsome stranger to a critical scrutiny. 'What about your work, Tessa?'

'I was talking about work when I said I'd been busy,' Tessa countered.

Oh, her mother could be so infuriatingly wicked! But she loved her dearly and felt guilty, as she always did, that she hadn't found the time to come home before now.

'Mum, this is Max Forster,' she said quickly, suddenly remembering her manners.

Max smiled as he shook her mother's hand. 'I've come to check out the oat cake situation, Mrs Grainger. Your daughter has got me hooked on them since I started working with her at the hospital.'

Oh, what a smoothy! Tessa thought as she saw the big smile spread across her mother's face.

'Dr Forster! I knew you looked familiar as soon as you walked in. You used to live over in Cragdale and Tessa here used to do a bit of babysitting for you, didn't she? But, oh—'

She broke off in mid-sentence, her facial expression showing her real concern at the sentiments of sympathy she'd been about to voice.

Turning away quickly, she said, 'I'll mash some tea.'

'It's OK, Mum, I'll do it,' Tessa said quickly, realising that her mother must have heard the sad news that Max was now a widower.

'I always thought this was a lovely farm when I used to come over to collect Tessa,' Max was saying as he looked up at the high ceiling. 'I'm living in an old house now and starting to collect antiques.'

'The sitting room's the place where we keep the best antiques,' Mrs Grainger told him, recovering some of her equilibrium as she set out the freshly baked oat cakes on a large pink-and-gold rimmed plate.

She pointed across the kitchen. 'Go through that door

there and have a look. We'll bring the tea through. Fred's lit the fire.'

Tessa picked up the heavy kettle from the hob in front of the fire. As she poured the boiling water onto the tea leaves she wondered why she had the feeling that her mother wanted a word in private.

'Poor man. What a tragic thing to happen, his wife dying like that,' Mrs Grainger whispered, as the door closed behind Max.

Tessa set the teapot on a tray and started lifting the cups and saucers down from their place on the second shelf of the cupboard. She remembered fleetingly how she'd always had to stand on a stool to reach them when she was a child.

'Yes, I was shocked when I heard about it,' she said, taking hold of the small milk jug. Someone had wedged it behind a pile of saucers.

'Terrible, wasn't it, Tessa! Driving off the edge of a cliff like that—it doesn't bear thinking about!'

It was seconds before Tessa realised that she'd knocked one of the saucers onto the stone floor. It broke into several pieces but she ignored it as she faced her mother.

'What did you say, Mum?'

Her mother's face was ashen. 'Nay, lass, don't tell me you didn't know?'

'Was it…was it an accident?'

Mrs Grainger was shaking her head.

'Nobody knows. There was a little bit in the local paper, him being from round here—well, having worked at the hospital, that is. Now, let me see what I can remember. You'd just started your nursing training so it must have been about twelve years ago. I didn't show you the paper because I thought it would upset you. I know you were fond of their little girl…what was she called?'

'Francesca,' Tessa replied automatically.

'I'll get the dustpan and brush so we can sweep up that mess. You're not usually clumsy like that. It must have been the shock of—'

'Why did you say nobody knows whether it was an accident? Surely…'

'I only know what it said in the *Moortown Echo*.'

'Which was?'

Mrs Grainger lowered her voice. 'The coroner out there in America recorded an open verdict. Doesn't that mean they don't know what happened?'

CHAPTER FIVE

MAX was admiring the miniature portraits hanging over the sitting-room fire. He looked calm and composed. The door to the sitting room had been shut to keep in the warmth of the log fire so he couldn't have heard Tessa talking to her mother—she hoped!

He turned when she came in with the teatray.

'Here, let me help you with that. It looks heavy.'

He took the tray from her.

She cleared a space on the coffee-table. 'I hope you're not suggesting my mother's oat cakes are heavy,' she quipped, as she tried to manufacture a cheerful expression.

The shock of her mother's revelation was still affecting her. She was regretting all the times she'd tried to shake Max out of himself. How did anybody get over a tragedy like that? The tragedy itself was bad enough but the fact that nobody knew the circumstances, why or how it had happened…

He put a hand on her arm. 'Shall I pour the tea? You look as if you've seen a ghost. Are you OK?'

She gave herself a little shake. 'I'm fine! I'll pour the tea. You sit down by the fire. Help yourself to an oat cake.'

'Isn't your mother going to join us?'

'My sister-in-law, Gemma, and the children have just got back from a walk and Mum's having tea in the kitchen with them. Felicity and Michael are only five and four. They make too much mess if they have tea in the sitting room.'

Her hand shook as she reached for the teapot, automatically lifting the lid and giving the leaves a good stir as her mother had taught her years ago in this very room.

He was watching her with an expression of concern. 'Yes, I thought I heard someone arriving.'

Tessa remembered how, a few minutes ago, she'd heard the sound of Gemma and the children out in the corridor as she'd knelt on the floor to sweep up the broken saucer. She'd pulled a tissue and dabbed furiously at her eyes, not wanting anyone to see how badly her mother's news had affected her.

Settling herself in the armchair at the other side of the fireplace, she experienced a deep feeling of compassion as she looked across at Max. He was biting into an oat cake, oblivious to her emotional turmoil. As if sensing her eyes on him, he glanced up.

'You're doing it again, Tessa. Looking at me as if you haven't seen me before. What's happened?' he said gently.

It was all too much for her. She crossed the hearthrug and knelt at his feet.

'I'm sorry I've been hounding you. I didn't realise that…'

'Hey, what's the matter?'

He bent down, stroking her hair. She turned to look up at him. His eyes were tender. In that instant she knew she was falling hopelessly in love with him. She wanted to help him—but not in the way she had been, relentlessly pursuing her own idea of how he should recover from his trauma.

'My mother thought I knew about the tragic way your wife died. Apparently, she read something about it in the local paper. She said…'

She couldn't go on.

His hand tightened on her shoulder. 'That Catherine's car went over a cliff?'

She sensed the pain beneath his even tone. He'd learned

to live with it in his own way. She had no right to disturb the calm he'd affected as a way of dealing with his grief.

She could hear children's voices out in the corridor. The kitchen tea was over. Her niece and nephew would burst in here any moment. She pulled herself to her feet just before the door opened and two smiling, blond-haired, blue-eyed children ran across to grab her round the legs.

'Can we stay in here and play with you, Aunty Tessa?' Michael said excitedly.

For the first time in her life Tessa didn't feel like playing with Michael and Felicity. They were an adorable pair but at that moment all she wanted to do was escape somewhere quiet to be alone with Max.

'How about a story?' she said hopefully. 'Just a short one because Max and I have to get back to hospital.'

'Are you a doctor?' Felicity said, gazing up at Max with trusting eyes.

He smiled down at her. 'Yes, I'm a doctor.'

Felicity put out her pudgy arms and asked to be lifted onto his knee.

'I went to the hospital when I was only four and a nice doctor mended my broken arm. I'm five now. That's why I'm bigger than Michael. When I'm properly grown up I'm going to be a doctor. Will you tell me a story about a doctor?'

Michael had joined his sister and had managed to squeeze himself up on to Max's other knee. Tessa sat down again in her armchair, leaning back against the cushions and enjoying the sight of Max entertaining her niece and nephew.

He was inventing a story about a magic doctor who could cure everything. Dr Magic could also make people laugh when they were sad and Tessa found herself laughing with the children at the outrageous antics of this amazing character who worked in a place called Happy Healing Hospital.

Twice Max tried to end the story but the children begged him to continue.

On the third occasion, when they were clamouring for more, her fair-haired sister-in-law, Gemma, walked in.

'That's enough, children.' She smiled at Max. 'Thank you so much for looking after them. They can be a handful but you've obviously had a lot of experience of children—I mean in hospital,' she added quickly.

Tessa sensed that her mother had managed to explain who Max was.

'I have one daughter, Francesca,' he said quietly. 'I used to tell her stories when she was small.'

He was standing up now, lifting the children gently from his lap.

'Will you come again?' the children asked, jumping up and down excitedly in front of him.

'Mr Forster is a very busy man,' their mother said quickly. 'But he's always welcome. Mum said you'd left your car up on the moors. Can I give you a lift back there?'

Could she! Tessa's calf muscles were stiffening up after sitting by the fire. The easier she could be transported back to hospital, the better.

Tessa was relieved that they didn't have to walk back up the steep path and across the moors. The sun was slanting down in the sky, the shadows were lengthening and a strong east wind had sprung up. It would have been decidedly chilly up there on the moors.

She waved goodbye to her sister-in-law who was manoeuvring her Jeep beside the stream. Max was waiting by his car, holding open the passenger door for her.

'I see what you meant about the track!' Gemma called through her open car window as she successfully negotiated her way around another rock, before engaging low gear to climb the hill.

'We suggested you leave us at the top!' Tessa shouted, cupping her hands round her mouth so that she would be heard above the noise of Gemma's Jeep engine and the rushing of the swollen stream.

Gemma waved a hand out of the car window. 'Next time I most definitely will! Bye!'

By the time Max had turned the car round and started up the hill, there was no sign of Gemma.

'She's a good sport, your sister-in-law,' he said, driving slowly between the large stones. 'This track looks as if it used to be a river-bed.'

Tessa laughed. 'I think it was during the winter.'

She was glad they'd spent those last few minutes with the children at the farm. The story interlude had lightened the tense atmosphere. If Max was able to function in that warm-hearted way when it was required, was she wrong to try and change him?

She stole a sideways glance at the strong, determined profile. Maybe he really had got his life sorted out.

She turned away and looked out of the side window at the darkening woods. The daisies, scattered in the grass, were closing their petals for the night. The trees which had looked so beautiful in the early afternoon sunlight now looked hostile and mysteriously dangerous.

She came to a decision. On the surface Max seemed as if he'd got his life sorted out, but not as far as she was concerned. She didn't want to spend time with a man who couldn't give himself one hundred per cent. She wasn't interested in a temporary physical fling.

So she was back to square one! To affect a change in Max's outlook, she'd have to be much more subtle than she had been. Use a kid glove instead of a hammer or else...

'Penny for them,' he said quietly, as he turned the wheel and drove on to the undulating moorland road.

She crossed her fingers. 'Oh, I'm not thinking about anything important. Nothing you'd be interested in.'

Not much!

It was two weeks since the picnic and the walk over the moors to the farm. The change in Max's attitude towards her had been noticeable in various small ways. Even Hannah remarked about it when they were working together in the obstetrics clinic.

It was while they were waiting for their final patient. They hadn't had a minute to spare all afternoon and, having successfully worked their way through the long list, Tessa was relieved to have a minute to catch her breath. But Hannah, with her family responsibilities, was getting impatient.

'If Rebecca Grayson doesn't turn up soon I'll have to leave her for Max to see.'

She leaned across the desk and gave Tessa a knowing smile. 'Good thing he's in a better mood these days.'

Tessa rolled her eyes. 'I'm sure I don't know what you mean, Hannah.'

'Pull the other one! Whatever treatment you're giving him it's certainly working.'

Tessa leaned back in the chair and pulled a wry face. 'There's a long way to go before—' She broke off in embarrassment.

'Before what, Tessa?'

Tessa took a deep breath. Hannah was the only person in this hospital in whom she could confide. And she needed to unburden herself.

'Before I'd consider having a real relationship with him,' she said, quietly.

'But I've seen you together off duty and you seemed to

be having a whale of a time. Only yesterday there you were shopping in the high street. You didn't see me so I didn't cross the street. You were laughing at something Max had said and I assumed you were…well, what I mean is, haven't you…?'

'We were buying a birthday present for Francesca.' Tessa hesitated. 'Max asked me to help him choose it. And, no, before you ask again, we haven't slept together and we're not likely to because—'

'Oh, come on, Tessa. You're not waiting for him to pop the question, are you? I mean, that sort of thing went out with—'

'No, of course I'm not!'

She was beginning to think she could do without Hannah's advice after all.

'I don't want to be there for Max's convenience whenever he's feeling sexy, to put it bluntly. He's had meaningless physical relationships before and ended them as soon as he got bored.'

'But it doesn't have to be a purely physical relationship, Tessa. From what I've seen, the pair of you have a wonderful rapport between you.'

'And that's how I want it to stay,' Tessa said, making the point rather too forcefully as she desperately tried to convince herself.

She turned to look at Hannah and gave her a sheepish grin. 'I think!' she added in a small, indecisive voice.

Hannah smiled. 'Exactly! I can tell what you want and it's not a platonic relationship. Stop holding yourself back, Tessa. If you're waiting for the love affair of your life, let me tell you—it will grow from what you and Max have already got between you.'

'Do you really think so?'

'I know so. You should have seen the obstacles Simon

and I had to surmount before we finally made it. Real love is never an easy option, but it's worth fighting for if…'

Hannah's words trailed away as the door opened. Max was standing in the doorway.

'Staff Nurse Phillips brought me a patient just before she went off duty. I've looked for the notes but I think you must have them, Hannah.'

Hannah picked up the file on her final patient. 'Rebecca Grayson? Rona should have brought her in here. We've been waiting for her.'

She gave Tessa a conspiratorial smile, indicating that she thought their waiting time had been well spent.

'Look, Max,' Hannah went on quickly, 'I really should get home. Simon's got a meeting and my housekeeper, Mrs Rainer, gets tired around teatime when she's had the kids all day. Would you see Rebecca Grayson for me?'

She glanced at Tessa. 'If Rona's gone off duty, Tessa will help, won't you?'

Tessa nodded, avoiding Max's eyes. How much had he heard when he'd walked in? Did he know the radical measures Hannah was advising?

'Goodbye, Hannah,' she said, as she followed Max across to his room.

Hannah was already shrugging out of her white coat, reaching for the jacket hanging at the side of the door. Her mind on the domestic matters that awaited her at home, she was probably unaware of what she'd stirred up.

Max turned at the door to his consulting room. 'Do you have to go back to the ward when we've finished with this final patient?'

She shook her head. 'I should have been off duty ten minutes ago. It's one of my rare evenings off.'

'Ah, yes, I remember you telling me you preferred to do

the handing over to the night staff yourself. Such dedication!'

'I love my work,' she countered, looking up at the enigmatic expression on his face.

'All work and no play makes—'

'Makes people rich and unhappy,' she improvised lightly. 'But not in my case. Because my salary doesn't change, however much work I do, and I'm very happy so…'

'What I was going to suggest was an evening over at my place. Francesca has a rehearsal for the school play and I'm going to be terribly lonely.'

She smiled at the uncharacteristically wheedling tone he was using.

'If you bring your toothbrush you could stay the night— in one of the guest rooms,' he added, with a rakish grin. 'As you know, there are two on the top floor so you'd be quite safe up there.'

She hesitated, her heart thumping.

'It would mean you could have two glasses of wine instead of one,' he went on quickly. 'And Francesca can bring you a cup of tea in the morning.'

'Ah, now you're talking!' She kept her tone light.

One of the cleaners, carrying a plastic bucket of water and a mop, squeezed past them.

'Will you be long, sir?' she asked, giving Max an impatient look.

'Only one lady to see, Betty. I'll give you a shout when we've finished.'

Their patient was a young woman with a mass of unruly golden hair and a friendly smile. She brushed aside Max's apologies for keeping her waiting.

'That's OK, Doctor. I've enjoyed sitting still, reading my magazine. I only flew in from Australia yesterday and I'm a bit jet-lagged.'

Max was scanning Rebecca Grayson's notes. 'What made you decide to have your baby in England, Mrs Grayson?'

'Oh, please, call me Becky. I persuaded my husband to come over because we were both born here. He's got an uncle who's given him a job on his sheep farm.'

'So you're planning to settle here in Yorkshire, are you?'

'Yes.' Becky paused, before continuing in a confidential tone. 'It's all about putting down roots,' she told them, gesturing with her hands in an animated way.

In fact, Tessa decided that Becky Grayson was one of those people who couldn't talk without moving her arms and hands. She looked as if she was a very lively character.

'When I said I was born here, I meant actually in this hospital—or so they tell me. That's about all the information my adoptive mother gave me last year just before she died. So I wanted to return and have my baby born here.'

Max began to make notes. 'Tell me about your general health, Becky.'

Tessa was fixing up the scanning machine while Max continued to take the case history notes. When he'd finished he asked Tessa to help Becky get ready for the scanning table.

'So you think you're about seven months, Becky?' Tessa said, as she smoothed the special scanning cream on her patient's swollen abdomen.

She saw a sheepish grin stealing over Becky's face. 'Actually, I'm nearer eight months. Thirty-six weeks, to be precise.'

Max's eyes widened. 'But what about the long flight from Australia? Didn't the airline check that—'

'They took the word of a doctor friend of mine who changed the date of my last period. I'm a trained nurse so I knew I was fit enough to fly. The reason I flew so late was because I wanted to work out my contract at the hospital and get as much money as I could before we left Australia.'

The image of the baby forming on the screen showed Tessa that this was indeed a thirty-six-week pregnancy.

'That looks as if you've only four more weeks to full term,' she said, her eyes on the screen. 'Have you been having antenatal care in Australia?'

'Yes, my friendly doctor kept up the pretence that I was a month less advanced,' Becky said, glancing up at Max.

'I expect you don't approve but—'

Max put a hand on the patient's arm. 'Becky, I'm here to take care of you. You've got here all in one piece and that's all that matters.'

Tessa removed the cream from Becky's abdomen with a piece of dry gauze. As soon as her patient was fully dressed and sitting back in the chair, Max started to take her blood pressure.

Tessa could see Becky watching the rise of the column of mercury on the sphygmomanometer which indicated how high her blood pressure was.

Frowning at the blood pressure reading in front of him, Max said, 'I'm sorry, Becky, but as a trained nurse, you'll agree with me that your blood pressure is much too high.'

'I was afraid it might be,' Becky said quietly. 'I've had blood-pressure problems for a few weeks.'

'The flight won't have helped,' Max said evenly.

He was rubbing his chin thoughtfully. 'It could settle in a few days, but I'll have to admit you so I can monitor the situation. We'll give you some medication to treat the problem and put you on complete bed rest for a few days.'

'Is it really necessary, Doctor?'

'Yes, I'm afraid it is,' Max said firmly. 'Sister Grainger will take you up to Nightingale Ward.'

'I'll ring for a wheelchair and a porter,' Tessa said. 'Don't worry, Becky. You're going to the best ward in the hospital. We pride ourselves in making it a real home from home.'

Max took Tessa to one side. 'Talking of home, I'd like to leave as soon as possible.'

So would she! Dedication to duty was all very well but a girl had to have her times for relaxation and whatever else was on the agenda tonight.

'I'll hand over the reins to my staff nurse as soon as I've settled Becky in.'

'Looks like Francesca's home,' Max said, moving the bag of books that had been dumped in the middle of the hall.

Tessa followed him into the kitchen.

Francesca looked up from turning the handle on the salad spinner. 'Tessa! What a lovely surprise. I didn't know you were coming to supper.'

Tessa smiled. 'Neither did I until the end of the afternoon. What happened about the play rehearsal?'

Francesca looked puzzled. 'It's tomorrow. It's always on—'

'Yes, of course it is,' Max interrupted. 'I'd read it wrong in my diary again.'

Tessa gave him a knowing smile. 'And I dashed off duty so that I could keep you company. As you can see, I've literally thrown myself into these old jeans and—'

'Oh, you look great,' Francesca said, lifting off the lid of the salad spinner and arranging the lettuce leaves in a large pottery bowl.

'To be honest, I was a bit scared of you when you turned up in that posh suit last time. I thought you might be like Vanessa and Carol. They always looked as if they'd come straight from the beauty shop and—'

She broke off and glanced at Max who was uncorking a bottle of wine.

'Sorry, Dad. I know you don't like me making fun of them but they really were a pain.'

Max gave his daughter a wry grin. 'I'll agree with you on that.'

He poured out a couple of glasses of wine and handed one to Tessa.

'Here's to casual dressing,' he said, raising his glass.

'Talking of dressing, Dad, will you mix the vinaigrette for the salad?' Francesca said, as she set the salad bowl in the middle of the kitchen table, before putting out the cutlery.

'I'll do it,' Tessa said quickly. 'Show me where you keep your oil and vinegar. And have you got some French mustard?'

'Everything's in this low cupboard,' Max said, leaning over her as she stooped to investigate.

The faint animal smell of his end-of-day perspiration mingled with the distinctive aroma of his aftershave. Her fingers pushed aside the jars and bottles as she tried to concentrate on the task in hand. He was lingering just a little too close and too long.

She turned, clutching the requisite jars and bottles in both hands. His eyes held an expression of real tenderness and something else—or was she imagining that look of expectancy? It was the kind of expression that said he was in no hurry but he was hoping for more.

They ate supper sitting around the kitchen table. Max had heated up a broccoli and Stilton soup that he'd made on the previous evening. Francesca produced the remains of a cold ham and some tomatoes to go with the dressed green salad and there was fresh fruit for dessert.

As Tessa was peeling herself an apple she was aware that Francesca was watching her with great interest.

'You've left the peel all in one piece,' Francesca remarked admiringly. 'I've always tried to do that ever since I was shown how to throw it over my shoulder on Hallowe'en night. Last October my apple peel made an S when it fell on the floor. And guess what? I met this really fantastic boy at the school disco and his name was Steve.'

'And?' Tessa said, smiling as she leaned towards Francesca.

Francesca gave a wry grin. 'And nothing. He bought me a Coke—a Coca-Cola, that is, Dad.'

Max smiled. 'I know what a Coke is, Francesca. I'm not that ancient!'

'I didn't want you to think I was into drugs because I'm not.'

'Of course you're not. Tell us more about the wonderful Steve,' Max said dryly.

Francesca shrugged. 'That's it. He bought me a Coke. We chatted for a bit and then he said he had to go home. That was last Christmas and I haven't seen him since.'

'Sounds like he made a big impression on you,' Tessa said thoughtfully. 'Was it just that his name began with an S so you assumed that…?'

'Oh, Tessa, don't subject the poor girl to a psychological questioning session.'

Max's tone was jocular but his eyes were deadly serious. He turned to look at his daughter. 'Tessa is keen on psychology.'

'So am I,' Francesca countered. 'I think it's fascinating, studying the working of the mind and what makes people tick. I might study to become a psychiatrist after I've got my general medical qualification.'

'Well, don't decide until you've gone through medical school,' Max said earnestly.

'Francesca's got plenty of time ahead of her,' Tessa said quickly, anxious to diffuse the tension.

Francesca pushed back her chair. 'I'd better get on with my homework. Will you come and see me before you go, Tessa?'

'Tessa's staying the night,' Max said. 'Would you check if there are clean towels in the pink guest room?'

'Sure.'

Tessa was pleased to see the happy smile that spread across Francesca's face. It was good to feel welcome.

'I'm tea monitor in the mornings,' Francesca said, turning at the door. 'Do you take sugar, Tessa?'

Tessa shook her head. 'No, thanks. Work well. I'll be up to see you later.'

The door closed. They were alone. Suddenly she felt uncharacteristically shy.

She half rose. 'I'll start on the dishes.'

'No,' he put out his hand. 'Leave them. I've been stacking the dishwasher as we went along. I'll finish off later.'

He picked up the cafetière. 'More coffee?'

'Please.'

She sat very still, listening to the sound of the ancient grandfather clock, ticking away in the corner of the kitchen. From somewhere out on the hillside she heard the bleating of a lamb.

'Another successful spring delivery, Max.'

He smiled as he listened to the welcome sound. 'Amazing how these sheep just get on with it! I love listening to all the animal sounds around here. It makes this house feel like a proper home.'

She took a sip of her coffee. 'You're quite domesticated, aren't you?'

He shrugged. 'Hobson's choice. As I told you before, I've always had to cook even when I was quite a young boy. And Catherine didn't like cooking so I used to take over when I wasn't working at the hospital.'

He paused, his eyes on her face, watching her reaction. 'Actually, I was the one who prepared your kitchen suppers on a tray when you were babysitting.'

Tessa smiled. 'Well, thank you. They were always very delicious. I used to look forward to them.'

'I was using the suppers as an incentive, if the truth be known. Good babysitters were a bit thin on the ground in Cragdale and you'd come highly recommended.'

She was intrigued. 'By whom?'

'Your father.'

She smiled. 'And it didn't occur to you that Dad might have been a bit biased in his opinion of his only daughter?'

Max grinned. 'I could tell he was a doting father but I was prepared to take his word. He said you were anxious to make a bit of pocket money. Funny how it's all coming back now that I've been seeing you again.'

'Where did you meet my father?'

'In the Moortown Athletics clubhouse. He used to run with the veterans. I was still running with the under-thirties when I could get the time off duty.'

He paused, watching her closely. 'Your dad seemed very fit for a man of his years.'

Tessa swallowed hard as the memories flooded back. 'Oh, he was until he ran one race too many. Mum was devastated when he collapsed in the half-marathon and they couldn't revive him.'

'It must have been awful for her—for all of you.'

The ticking of the clock seemed louder as she tried to banish the memories.

'It was…but life goes on.'

He reached across and covered her hand with his. 'I'm waiting.'

She stared at him. 'For what?'

'For you to tell me to shake myself out of it. All your psychobabble about—'

She snatched back her hand. 'It isn't psychobabble! I really would like to help you. I honestly think you've been in mourning for Catherine for far too long. It's time—'

'It's not Catherine I'm mourning,' he said quietly.

She put down her cup and leaned forward, not sure whether she'd heard what he'd said.

'What do you mean?'

He placed the tips of his fingers together and studied them in the characteristic manner she'd seen him use so often when he was deep in thought.

She waited, watching him, not daring to break the silence.

He moistened his lips. When he finally spoke, his voice was a mere whisper.

'To give all that love and then be disillusioned is the thing I regret most.'

She felt as if the hairs on the back of her neck were standing up. 'Disillusioned?'

He put his fingers flat on the wooden table and looked across at her. His eyes were wide as if he'd forgotten she was there.

'Did I say disillusioned?'

She nodded. 'Yes. Why did you say it?'

'That's the first time I've admitted it to myself,' he began, his voice husky with emotion, 'but, yes, after I'd come to terms with the hurt, it was the unrelenting disillusion that haunted me. I knew I could never live at that level of emotional intensity again. Not if it was to end like that.'

She moved round the table, pulling a chair close to him. Placing her hands on his arms, she looked directly into his eyes.

'Max, it was good while it lasted so—'

'You saw us in our happy phase. Before Catherine started playing around.'

'I'm sorry. I didn't know that…'

He ran a hand through his dark hair. His eyes held a haunted expression.

'I was working long hours when we went over to America, climbing the hospital ladder as quickly as I could, trying to increase my salary to keep pace with the expensive lifestyle that Catherine wanted.'

He closed his eyes briefly and then opened them again, staring up at the ceiling but obviously seeing nothing except his memories.

'The trouble was that Catherine had too much time on her hands. She joined a health club. Wayne was her swimming coach. He seemed a nice enough young man. I didn't suspect a thing.'

She saw the beads of sweat standing out on his forehead.

'Look, Max, if you'd rather not tell me about—'

'I'm OK. I've never told anyone the whole story before.'

She waited. They were sitting so close she imagined she could hear his heart beating. He pulled impatiently at his tie and threw it onto the back of a chair.

Leaning forward, she loosened the collar of his shirt.

'Thanks. I should have changed out of this damn suit when I came in. Now, where was I?'

'You were telling me about Catherine and—'

'It's a long story. Let's get comfortable.'

He pushed back his chair and took hold of her hand. She allowed herself to be led into the sitting room. The empty grate of the fireplace had been filled with a large vase of daffodils.

He pushed the vase to one side of the hearth, before producing a packet of firelighters and some sticks from the depths of the log basket.

Striking a match, he tossed it on to the hastily assembled logs.

'Flowers are OK but fire is better when you need a bit of comfort.'

He joined her on the sofa, placing an arm on the back of the cushions, not quite touching her but infinitely disturbing. She watched the flickering of the infant flames as she waited for the denouement of his story, not daring to disturb the flow of what would surely be a harrowing account.

'As I was saying, Catherine had too much time on her hands after Francesca started nursery school. She didn't have any hobbies so she spent a lot of time in the beauty shop. Then she joined the health club where she met Wayne.'

Tessa was beginning to feel a growing animosity towards this woman whom she'd always thought had been near-perfect. Catherine hadn't been able to cook, hadn't driven well, hadn't had any hobbies and now Tessa was hearing that she'd been two-timing Max.

'Why was it that you once told me that Catherine was one in a million?' she asked quietly.

'Because I thought she was…until…' He took a deep breath, moving his arm from the back of the sofa to Tessa's shoulders. She relaxed against him as he pulled her against his side.

'Until I came home unexpectedly,' he said, his voice devoid of emotion. 'I'd been away at a weekend medical conference. We finished earlier than expected on the Sunday morning. I decided to skip the lunch and get home to Catherine and Francesca.'

His arm around her shoulder tightened. 'I'd left my car at home and taken a cab. It was such a lovely day I asked the cabbie to drop me on the other side of the park so that I could walk through and surprise them. I came into the house through the side gate. There was something floating just under the surface of the swimming pool.'

'Was it…?' Tessa held her breath and waited for Max to continue.

'It was Francesca. My precious little four year old had been left to play on her own while Catherine and the boyfriend were upstairs.'

Catherine clapped a hand over her mouth to stifle the cry that escaped her lips.

'I thought Francesca was dead. Her eyes were open but she seemed lifeless. I jumped in the pool, swam over, pulled her out and started working on resuscitating her—mouth-to-mouth, cardiac massage, frantically working and working until…'

He let out a sigh. 'Until she started spluttering and began breathing again. I picked her up in my arms and ran into the house to phone for an ambulance. Wayne was coming down the stairs, shoes in one hand, buttoning his shirt. Catherine was peeping over the landing, holding the sides of her lacy negligee together.'

For several seconds he remained silent. Tessa could see the dreadful images were still flashing across his mind.

'My priority was to get Francesca to hospital so I allowed the little rat to scuttle out of my house. But later that evening, when I knew Francesca was going to survive, I told Catherine exactly what I felt about her.'

She saw a pulse jumping in his temple as he struggled to describe what had happened on that fateful evening.

'I was beside myself with anger. I told her that Francesca could have died. Looking back, I shouldn't have said all the things I did but—'

'Of course you should! Catherine deserved more than a ticking-off. She—'

'I blame myself,' he said quietly, 'for what happened after that.'

'What did happen?'

He took a deep breath. 'Catherine started screaming at me, said she couldn't stand it when I got angry. She went out to her car and climbed in. I should have gone after her. She was a terrible driver...but I let her go.'

'You weren't to know that she would—'

'Drive over the cliff?'

His voice was a bare, hoarse whisper, delivered in a tone of infinite resignation.

'They recorded an open verdict. Nobody knows if she intended to do it or if she simply put her foot on the accelerator when she meant to put it on the brake. It was a beautiful view from the top—we'd often gone up there to watch the sunset.'

He turned towards her, putting one finger under her chin so that she had to look up into his eyes.

'If I hadn't introduced her to the place, if I hadn't shouted at her, she'd still be alive.'

'Life's full of ifs! You can't go on blaming yourself, Max. If Catherine hadn't two-timed you...'

The door was opening. Tessa stopped in mid-sentence.

Francesca stood on the threshold, looking into the room with doleful eyes.

'It's OK. I guessed what happened a long time ago. I knew Mum had been unfaithful. People think kids don't understand but...'

Max stood up and went over to his daughter. 'Who told you, Francesca?'

'I was listening in one day to a couple of mums after school. I must have been about seven at the time, I suppose—old enough to gather what they were talking about. And I remembered the man who used to bring me sweets.

And the day I woke up in hospital with everybody fussing around me.'

Max put an arm round his daughter's shoulders.

'They said you must have had a big row about her having the affair. They said that was why she killed herself.'

Tessa saw the look of pure anguish that crossed Max's face.

'That's only one theory,' Tessa said quickly. 'It could have been an accident.'

'We'll never know what happened,' Francesca said quietly.

'It's all in the past,' Tessa said. 'You've got a wonderful life ahead of you, Francesca.'

'Yes, I know.' Francesca squeezed her father's hand. 'I'm tired, so I'm going to go to bed. Will you both come up to say goodnight?'

Tessa smiled. 'Of course. Would you like a drink? Cocoa, hot chocolate?'

Her heart was brimming over with compassion for this child who'd had to grow up so quickly. She was half-adult now, but still the little girl she'd taken care of all those years ago.

'Hot chocolate would be nice, but only if you'll drink some with me.'

'We'll all have some,' Max said. 'I'll heat the milk. Why don't you two go along and I'll bring it upstairs?'

Tessa turned to look at him. 'Are you OK?'

He nodded. 'Go on upstairs. Francesca needs you.'

She hurried out of the room, catching up with Francesca on the landing.

Francesca put out a hand and took hold of Tessa's.

'Thanks for being here, Tessa. Both Dad and I have been bottling things up for far too long. It's such a relief to bring it all out in the open.'

She pushed open her bedroom door and turned to look at Tessa.

'You know, I've always pretended I couldn't remember my early childhood—for Dad's sake.'

CHAPTER SIX

TESSA sat on the edge of Francesca's bed and looked across at Max on the other side. He was cradling his mug of hot chocolate, seemingly listening to his daughter's account of the plot of *Pride and Prejudice*, the school play. But Tessa could see that he was miles away, over the ocean, years ago, still reliving that fateful day that had changed his life for ever.

She took another sip from her mug. Max had made it too sweet but she told herself it was the thought that counted. Max had made it specially for her so she'd drink it and tell him another time how she hated sugar.

Looking at him now, she felt herself consumed with real love and she knew that the emotions she was experiencing had nothing to do with physical desire.

Oh, that was still hidden away deep down, waiting to be triggered at the least touch of his hand, but it was a feeling of wanting to share his grief and pain, to be with him in the bad times as well as the good. Her love for Max was growing by the minute and there was nothing she could do about it—except hope that he would one day feel the same way about her.

Sitting here on the edge of the bed, she had the warm, cosy feeling that they were a real family—just the three of them. Since Max had arrived with the hot drinks Francesca hadn't spoken any more about the discussion they'd had downstairs and Tessa didn't intend to bring up the subject again unless Francesca started asking questions.

Max stretched his arms, gave a yawn and pulled himself up from the patchwork quilt.

'Don't you think it's time you went to sleep, Francesca? We wouldn't want you to be too tired to be brilliant at the rehearsal tomorrow evening. After all, you are the star of the show.'

Francesca giggled. 'I'm only playing Elizabeth. She's an easy character to understand and I know my words already so…'

'Elizabeth is a very important character in the play,' Tessa said. 'You need your sleep.'

'Will you come and see me in it, Tessa?'

'Of course, I will—if I'm free,' Tessa added quickly.

'Goodnight, Dad.'

Francesca turned and fixed her big brown eyes on Tessa. 'Can you spare me another minute? There's something I want to ask you.'

As Tessa watched Max going out of the door, she was apprehensively hoping that she'd be able to give the right answers to Francesca's question.

But she needn't have worried. She was relieved to find it had nothing to do with their previous conversation.

'It's my birthday next month and Dad asked me what I wanted as a present.'

Tessa was just about to say they'd already bought it, but realised that would have given the show away.

'I told him I'd seen this brilliant sweater in the new boutique down the high street. It's absolutely fabulous. Cashmere, would you believe? Dad gives me a clothes allowance so that I can buy my own things but it doesn't run to cashmere. So I thought for a special birthday present I could ask. I've always wanted…'

Tessa was trying to keep a straight face as she listened, knowing that the sweater in question was hidden away, wrapped in tissue paper in a fancy box somewhere in the house.

'I've always wanted something made of cashmere. It's bound to be expensive. Dad said he'd look into it but he couldn't promise anything.'

She paused and gave a wry grin. 'Thing is, I don't think he'll have the nerve to go into the place because it's got all sorts of flimsy underwear in the window.'

'I know the place you mean. What colour is…?'

'It's a sort of unusual shade of caramel. They had it in the middle of the window and now it's gone. Somebody must have…'

Tessa remembered how the snooty lady in the boutique had struggled to lift the sweater out of the window.

'It's part of my display. Wouldn't you consider another colour, madam?' she'd said.

'No, it's got to be that one in the window,' Max had persisted.

'I'll see if they have another one inside the shop, Francesca,' Tessa said solemnly. 'Caramel, you say?'

'Mmm, it's to go with my new cream-coloured trousers. Dad will give you the money if you tell him it's for my birthday.'

Tessa stood up. 'Time we were both asleep. Goodnight, Francesca.'

She almost said, Sweet dreams, but decided it wasn't appropriate tonight. After their harrowing discussion it would be preferable not to dream at all.

Down in the kitchen Max was putting the last of the dishes into the dishwasher. He slammed the dishwasher door shut and turned to look at her as she went in.

'I came to say goodnight, Max.'

He moved towards her. 'I hoped you would but I thought

you might have had enough and gone straight up to your room. You're a devil for punishment.'

He put both hands on the sides of her arms and stood looking down into her eyes.

'Enough? Max, I needed to know!'

'I didn't mean to unburden myself like that. It just sort of flowed out once I got going. You're a very sympathetic person to talk to, Tessa.'

She smiled. 'So you don't object to my psychobabble?'

Max raised an eyebrow. 'In small doses, some of it can be helpful. Anyway, I'm glad you know the whole story because now you can see what I'm up against. If only I could get rid of this feeling of guilt I—'

'Shh!' Tessa put her finger against his lips. 'Don't upset yourself. As I told Francesca, it's all in the past and you've got a brilliant future ahead of you.'

He pulled her close to him, wrapping his arms around her in a friendly bear hug. 'Mmm, you're so good for me.'

She remained still, resting her head against his shoulder. She sensed they were simply embracing like good friends who shared a secret together. He was seeking comfort as he'd done when he'd lit the fire that evening even though the sitting room had been perfectly warm.

She realised as he cradled her in his arms that she was a substitute for his fire. That was her function at the moment so very soon she'd extricate herself from his arms, go upstairs to her room and...

He was turning her face towards his, his expression vivid with a tender longing. Gently, oh, so gently, he lowered his head and kissed her, with a slow, sensuous movement of his lips.

She felt the dormant passion, deep down inside her, awakening with a liquid rush of excitement. His kiss deepened into a tantalising sensation that was removing the last vestige of her control. She strained against him, longing for more than just a mere embrace.

As he scooped her up into his arms she knew he'd read her thoughts. He'd recognised that she wanted him as much as he wanted her.

'I'm not as light as you think,' she whispered as he carried her out of the door.

He gave a carefree laugh as he nuzzled his head against her hair.

'Ever the practical one! You're light as a feather but I'll never make it to your room on the second landing. It will have to be my place not yours.'

She closed her eyes as if to extinguish reality. Clasping her hands around his neck, she allowed herself to be carried up the stairs. Her mounting excitement had banished all thoughts of whether this made sense. All she knew was that she wanted to make love with Max. Only the present mattered and she'd think about tomorrow when it came…

Tessa was aware of the sound of birds cheeping loudly. Slowly she opened her eyes, wondering when birds had started nesting outside her window in the nurses' home. Looking up at the lush, richly draped crimson canopy of the four-poster bed, she remembered where she was.

Glancing sideways, she saw that Max was propped up on one elbow, watching her, a contented smile on his face. She smiled back and he leaned over to kiss her.

He was naked. She could see the gleam of sweat on his chest, mingling with the dark hairs. She put out her hand and touched him, almost shyly, as if to reassure herself he was real.

What should she say to this man who'd given her so much pleasure during a night devoted to love and passion? Should she try a variation of the well-used cliché, How was it for you?

She almost shuddered with embarrassment at the thought. Better not to say anything, but simply bask in the expression of his eyes which told her more than mere words could ever do.

'It was the birds that woke me,' she said.

'They're house martins who've made their nests under the eaves outside the window. They always waken me around the same time every morning.'

He leaned back against the pillows. 'Much better than an alarm clock. More romantic, don't you think?'

Everything about Max's bedroom was romantic as far as she was concerned, from the thick, cream, woollen carpet to the crimson and gold floor-length curtains. She would have liked to have stayed there all day, but she realised that she would have to start being practical again.

'I'd better go to the upstairs bedroom,' she said, lifting herself upright from the pillows. 'Francesca will—'

'Not yet,' he murmured, pulling her into his arms. 'Stay just a few minutes longer.'

She made a feeble effort to remind Max of the time, but as his hands roamed over her already roused body she gave in to the irresistible temptation...

Coming up for air, she ran her hand over his forehead. This final act had left her breathless, with her senses reeling, for their love-making got better every time they came together. During the night she'd thought they couldn't find out anything more about each other but she'd been wrong!

Glancing at the clock she leapt out of bed before Max could hold onto her. Shrugging herself into his huge towelling robe, she gathered up her clothes from the heap on the floor. Quietly she opened the door and ran barefoot over the soft carpet up to the top floor.

Which was the pink room? She couldn't remember from the brief tour that Francesca had given her when she'd first come to the house. When she'd located it she dumped her crumpled clothes on a chair and went into the pretty, flower wallpapered bathroom.

It was only when she was climbing out of the scented bath that she remembered she hadn't ruffled the sheets on the bed.

Too late! There was a knocking on the door, followed by the sound of it opening.

'I've put your tea on the bedside table, Tessa,' she heard Francesca calling.

'Thanks very much.'

As she heard the door closing again, she reflected that the cat was well and truly out of the bag! But maybe Francesca would think she'd made the bed before she had her bath?

No chance! Returning to her bedroom, she saw the spare towels which Francesca had placed on her bed, the covers of which had been neatly turned down ready for her to jump in.

Sipping her tea, she comforted herself with the thought that Francesca was no longer a child. She was almost sixteen and had been forced to grow up quickly. But she didn't want Francesca to think that she was going to be just another of her father's concubines like Vanessa or Carol. Because she wasn't—was she?

The awful thought sent shivers of apprehension running through her. Was it possible that Max would simply regard her as someone to ease his physical tension? Would he tire of her and cast her off like he had done with—?

'Breakfast!'

Max's voice floated up the stairs, followed by the loud banging of the brass gong she'd seen standing in the hall.

After this she heard peals of laughter from Francesca as she proceeded to bang the gong for longer than was necessary. Good! The girl was in high spirits so she couldn't be feeling upset at discovering that Tessa had slept with Max.

As she walked down the ward, adjusting the cuffs of her uniform, Tessa had the feeling that all eyes must be upon her. Surely it must be obvious from her more than usually fluid movements that she was in love. Today she felt like a ballet dancer as her feet covered the distance between her office and the antenatal section of Nightingale.

She stopped beside Becky Grayson's bed and smiled down at her newly admitted patient. Was is it really only a few hours since yesterday's obstetric clinic? It seemed like a whole lifetime ago!

'Just going to check on your blood pressure, Becky,' Tessa said, glancing at Becky's charts. 'Hmm, still much too high.'

She unfurled the cuff of the sphygmomanometer. Fixing the cuff around Becky's arm she started to pump up the column of mercury, listening carefully through the special plugs in her ears. She was concentrating so hard that she didn't notice Max arriving on the other side of the bed.

Removing the earplugs, she looked up and felt herself blushing furiously. A grown woman and she was behaving like a teenager!

Max, obviously noticing her heightened colour, gave her a wickedly knowing smile before he turned to talk to their patient.

Putting away the blood pressure equipment she had time

to pull herself together and concentrate on being professional.

'Any improvement in the reading, Sister?' Max asked.

She shook her head. 'I'm afraid not, sir.'

She handed Max the charts and he studied them with deep concentration.

'We'll give this medication time to show some results,' he said evenly. 'If your situation doesn't improve, Becky, I'll have to change your medication.'

'Besides the medication, it's most important that you rest completely,' Tessa said. 'Try not to worry about anything.'

Becky smiled. 'I'm not the worrying kind, Sister.'

'I'm glad to hear it. Some of my patients never stop worrying.'

She glanced across the ward at Helen Cooper, who was frantically trying to catch her attention. She'd have to go across and reassure her again that she wasn't going to lose her precious baby.

She'd been relieved to find that all the recent tests on Helen had showed that the baby was getting as much nourishment as required even though the placenta was still slightly displaced where it joined the womb.

'I bet my mother worried when she had me,' Becky said. 'Poor soul. My adoptive mother told me that my birth mother was only fifteen when I was born. Can you imagine the social stigma in those days, not to mention the actual birth for a young schoolgirl. I expect I inherited this high blood pressure from her.'

'Yes, high blood pressure is often a constitutional condition,' Max agreed. 'And you were actually born in this hospital, you told me?'

'As far as I know. Do you know if the records go back twenty-two years? It could even have been in this very ward.'

'Nightingale Ward has been the obstetrics and gynaecology ward for about twenty-five years so it would have been here,' Tessa said, feeling a mounting interest in Becky's story. 'But we don't keep records for more than fifteen years so…'

'Pity. 'Cos when I get out of here one of the first things I'm going to do is try to trace my birth mother.'

'It doesn't always turn out to be a good idea, Becky,' Max cautioned gently. 'But if it's what you really want to do I can put you in touch with the people who deal with that sort of search.'

Becky smiled. 'Thanks a lot.'

'Sister!'

Tessa smiled reassuringly across the ward at Helen Cooper who was now waving her arms in agitation.

'I'm coming.' She turned back to Becky. 'Got to go and see Helen. She's so worried that something might happen to her baby. If you get a chance, give her a cheery word, will you? Or just the occasional smile would help.'

'Why don't you bring Helen over here, Sister?' Becky asked. 'You could put her in this empty bed next to me. I could do with a bit of company myself.'

Tessa smiled. 'Good idea. I'll arrange it as soon as I've had a chat with her.'

'I've got a long list in Theatre, this morning, Sister,' Max said, folding up the case notes and placing them back in the holder at the end of Becky's bed.

She watched him striding off down the ward. Yes, he looked different, too, this morning. She wondered if anyone else had noticed.

It took only minutes to reassure Helen that her baby's heart was still beating strongly and that her own health was actually improving since she'd been admitted to

Nightingale. As to the idea of moving across the ward, Helen wasn't sure she wanted to go.

'I've got used to being on this side, Sister, and—'

'Becky would really like to have somebody to chat with,' Tessa said quickly.

Helen smiled, pleased at being needed. 'Oh, well, in that case…'

'I'll ask Staff Nurse to move you, Helen. I've got to go and see some more patients.'

Walking away from the bed, Tessa congratulated herself on her diplomacy. Both Helen and Becky would benefit from having someone to take their minds off their problems. And they had a lot in common. Helen had given a baby up for adoption and Becky had been adopted so…

She stopped stock-still in the middle of the ward and clapped a hand to her mouth. Supposing…just supposing Helen was… No, it would be too much of a coincidence. It was just her fanciful mind playing tricks with her.

She made a determined effort to put the idea from her mind as she carried on with her ward round.

'Good morning, ladies,' she said to Jill and Josie. 'How are we today?'

Josie smiled and patted the large bump beneath her nightdress. 'We've just been comparing bumps and my triplets' bump is bigger than Jill's twins' bump even though she's a month further on than I am.'

Tessa smiled, pleased that the good relationship between these two patients was helping them to get through the final weeks of waiting.

'Just think how big I'm going to be when I'm at Jill's stage!' Josie continued, pulling a wry face. 'They'll need a crane to get me to the delivery room.'

Jill laughed. 'I'm sure that can be arranged, can't it, Sister?'

'Oh, absolutely!'

She studied Jill's charts. Blood pressure normal. The twins' heartbeats strong and regular.

'Did Samantha come in to see you yesterday evening, Jill? I wasn't on duty so—'

'We noticed you'd abandoned us. Go anywhere nice? Or more to the point, with anybody nice?'

Tessa could feel the colour rising in her cheeks. 'Had supper with some friends,' she said quickly.

'That's nice,' Jill said, glancing across the gap between the beds at Josie.

Tessa saw the knowing smile. She fervently wished she was one of those sophisticated women who could have a night of wild passion without having the signs stamped all over her!

'Yes, Samantha came to see me,' Jill continued happily. 'I told her she could take the twins home with her because they were kicking me to pieces but she decided to leave them a bit longer. I'll be thrilled to get rid of this load, I can tell you.'

Tessa smiled and patted her hand. 'Not much longer. Mr Forster was saying we'd probably deliver you at eight months.'

'Thank God for that!'

Josie's charts were equally encouraging, but to be on the safe side Tessa pulled round the curtains and made a thorough examination of her patient.

The precious triplets, which would be Josie's entire family, since this pregnancy was her last attempt, were in excellent health.

'Glad to hear it, Sister,' Josie said when Tessa told her the good news. She lowered her voice. 'I like being next to Jill, but I never tell her when I'm worried. We just crack a joke together and I tell myself to snap out of it.'

'Well, it certainly seems to work,' Tessa said.

She spent the rest of the morning in the postnatal section of her ward, examining her patients, chatting about their problems and helping with feeding.

Feeding a dear little boy of four days with a bottle of his mother's expressed breast-milk, she reflected that this was one of the perks of her job. To look down at the sweet, trusting face as the little rosebud mouth sucked noisily on the bottle's teat was very satisfying.

Young Harry had been delivered by Caesarean section and his mother was still too weak to feed him herself. The nursing staff had taken over Harry's feeding, sometimes giving him milk formula but whenever possible letting him feed on his mother's expressed breast milk.

Tessa lifted the baby over her shoulder and rubbed his back. She could sense the trapped wind rising until he gave a satisfying explosive burp.

'Good boy, Harry!'

She looked at his mother who had been lying on her side, watching.

'Do you want to give Harry a cuddle, Stephanie?' she asked, noticing the worry lines on her patient's pale forehead.

This fifth child, coming late in life, had been difficult for Stephanie, and she'd been sterilised at the same time as her Caesarean operation was performed to ensure that her health didn't suffer with further unplanned pregnancies.

'Yes, let me hold him for a bit, Sister,' her patient said. 'I need to get to know my youngest—and my last,' she added with a wry smile that crinkled up the lines on her face. 'You were a real pain, my lad, but you were worth it.'

Tess left Harry in his mother's arms, giving instructions to her staff nurse to put him back in his cot in a few minutes so that Stephanie wouldn't get tired.

Back in her office, she made a start on her day report. It was best to write things down as they happened and not wait until the late evening when she was always tired and might forget something. Besides, she was going to have an early night tonight. She was definitely short of sleep.

The door opened. She sensed it was Max even before she looked up. He was still in his theatre greens but was pulling off his theatre cap.

'Got to go back to Theatre as soon as possible. Phil paged me—said there was an emergency patient being admitted to Nightingale and—'

Tessa frowned. 'First I've heard about it.'

Through the open door she saw a stretcher arriving. Phil Dixon, their tall, young, thin, angular houseman was standing beside it, wearing his usual alert expression.

'I called you, Sister, but your ward phone was engaged.' He turned to Max. 'Thanks for coming, sir.'

Tessa was on her feet, out through the door and looking down at her new patient. Taking hold of the young woman's hand, she noticed immediately from the feel of her hot skin that she had a very high temperature.

'My provisional diagnosis is an ectopic pregnancy,' Phil told Tessa quietly.

The diagnosis was confirmed when Tessa assisted Max to examine their patient. The three-month pregnancy was indeed taking place in one of the Fallopian tubes. The fertilisation of the egg had taken place in the tube that led to the womb.

And from the signs and symptoms she'd observed she knew there was a real danger that the tube would rupture, causing dangerous complications.

Tessa administered a sedative and painkilling drug. Max took a sample of blood to determine the patient's blood group before fixing up a glucose saline drip.

The sedative was taking effect. Tessa felt relief when she saw her patient close her eyes. She could tell the pain was very severe.

'I'll operate immediately,' Max said, calling for the porter who was waiting outside to help him with the trolley. 'It will mean the next patient on my list will have to wait, but that case isn't an emergency like this one.'

'I'll prepare a post-operative bed for when she gets back here,' Tessa said, watching anxiously as Max, his face tense, began to move their patient.

Tessa sat down on the edge of her bed in the nurses' home and kicked her shoes off. She would give herself an hour before she went back on the ward for the evening session. Although she should have taken three hours off duty this afternoon, she'd been reluctant to leave the ward.

Theatre days were always busy and this one had been exceptionally so. Max had looked exhausted when he'd come to do a post-operative check on Pauline Scott, their ectopic patient. His surgical list had lasted well into the afternoon.

Max had told Tessa that he'd had to remove the affected Fallopian tube from Pauline.

Just before Tessa had come over to the nurses' home for her short break her patient had started to come round from the anaesthetic, but she was still too groggy to ask questions or understand answers.

Tessa wanted to be back on the ward when the inevitable sadness at losing her baby hit Pauline with full force. She'd had a great deal of experience at helping with patients' sorrow after operations like this.

Stretching out on the bed, she put her head back on the pillow. Mmm, if she wasn't careful she'd fall asleep but she mustn't...

The phone was ringing. Through the window she could see the lengthening shadows of the building opposite. She grabbed the phone.

'Mr Forster is asking for you, Sister.'

She recognised Staff Nurse Anne Reeve's voice.

'Be right with you.'

Max was in her office when she arrived, breathless. She closed the door.

'What's the problem, Max? Is it Pauline Scott? Has she—?'

'Hey, steady on. Catch your breath. There's no problem, at least nothing that we can't handle. Pauline's taken it quite well. She's fully round from the anaesthetic so we had a long chat. I told her that her remaining Fallopian tube was healthy so she'd be able to have another baby when she was ready. She's still young and strong.'

Tessa felt relieved that Max had been able to comfort Pauline even though she'd have preferred to be there when her patient needed reassurance.

'I'll go in to see her when I've got myself organised.'

He raised an eyebrow. 'I wondered what had happened to you. I came on the ward to check on my post-operative patients and noticed that our usually punctilious sister was missing.'

She sat down at her desk and started riffling through the latest lab reports which had been piled up on her desk. Her half-written report was still awaiting completion.

'I hate being late.'

'What kept you?'

She looked up and their eyes met. It was the first time that day that they'd been alone. She felt as if her heart was beginning to do a little dance.

'Leave that and come over here, Tessa,' he said, his tone languid and inviting.

'I've got to get these sorted before—'

He crossed the room and took her hands from the reports pulling her to her feet. She felt the churning of her emotions again as his breath fanned her face.

'What kept you?' he repeated gently.

'I fell asleep,' she said quietly.

He gave her a rakish grin. 'You must have been very tired, Sister.'

It was impossible to stay professional with Max holding her in his arms again.

'In fact, you must have been exhausted,' he carried on, in the same, relentlessly teasing manner. 'Were you out late last night, Sister?'

She laughed. 'Max, let me go! Someone might come in and…'

He pulled himself back, but still held onto her loosely. His eyes registered that he was enjoying himself.

'And would you mind if we were found in a compromising situation?'

'I…I don't know. I haven't had time to think it through…since last night, I mean.'

He dropped his hands to his side and stared at her. 'What is there to think through? You make it sound like a military manoeuvre. We had a wonderful time and—'

'I know, I know!'

She walked away from him over to the window. Below in the courtyard ambulance doors were being opened. Her life in this hospital world was whirling along too fast.

She turned back to face him.

'Where are we going, Max…you and I?'

She saw the puzzled frown appear on his face. 'What do you mean?'

'I'm an intensely practical person. I can't just drift along from day to day. I need to know if there's any future for us…together.'

'Why don't we take it one day at a time?' he said slowly.

'You mean, without commitment? No strings?'

He followed her over to the window, putting his finger under her chin and tilting her face up towards his.

'That way nobody gets hurt, Tessa,' he said huskily.

'You mean there's no chance of becoming disillusioned if you remain detached from a relationship, don't you?'

He bent his head and kissed her on the lips. The touch of his lips weakened her resolve. She held her breath as he raised his head again.

'Don't put words in my mouth, Tessa. Like I said, let's take it one day at a time. We've got something very special between us. Don't try to analyse what it is. Just accept it as a precious gift and enjoy it.'

'While it lasts?'

'I didn't say that. I…'

The door was opening. Tessa put a hand up to fix her cap as she moved towards her desk.

Staff Nurse Anne Reeves, the soul of discretion, kept her eyes averted from Max who was tapping his fingers impatiently on the window-sill.

'Pauline Scott is asking for you, Sister.'

Tessa shot her cuffs over her sleeves. 'I'm on my way.'

CHAPTER SEVEN

TESSA could smell the May blossom on the trees in the nurses' home garden as she hurried across to the hospital for breakfast. There was no need to wear her black, red-lined cloak any more. Winter was past, thank goodness.

As she looked up at the clear blue sky she wondered if Max would still be lying in bed, listening to the house martins outside his window. It seemed a lifetime since she'd lain in his arms that morning, the nerve endings beneath her skin still deliciously sensitive and her senses instantly aroused by the mere touch of his tantalising fingers.

A siren screamed and an ambulance pulled into the parking bay. She stood to one side to allow a stretcher to be carried in through the main door. She saw that the patient was a man so he wouldn't be coming up to Nightingale. She still had time for a quick breakfast before taking the report from the night staff.

Hurrying along the corridor she reflected ruefully that she must have frightened Max off. Yes, that was what it was. And who could blame him? She'd practically given him an ultimatum. If only she could have drifted along from day to day, as he'd suggested.

But she knew she couldn't. Life had to make sense for her and it would have been senseless to go along with the flow of passion only to have Max end it when he felt like it.

But would he have done that? She'd never know. She'd nipped it all in the bud.

She felt a hand on her shoulder and swung round. Max

was nearly out of breath as he smiled down at her. She reeled at the heady hint of his indefinable morning aroma, a combination of warm shower, scented, masculine soap, aftershave...

'I've been running to catch up with you. I was parking the car when I saw you going in through the door. Haven't had chance for a private word for ages.'

She was trying desperately to remain calm, even though her pulses were racing and her wretched cheeks were starting to flush.

'What about?'

She remained absolutely still, willing herself to stay in control of her churning emotions.

'It's Francesca's birthday today and...'

'I know. I've sent her a card. I've got a present for her in my office so if you'd like to call in and take it...'

'We'd really prefer it if you came for supper tonight. She's having a party at the local disco on Saturday with all her friends but tonight will seem a bit flat if we don't have some kind of celebration. She asked me at breakfast to try and get you to come.'

She looked up at his earnest expression. He could have asked her before.

She hesitated. 'It's very short notice. I'm not sure if I can make it.'

He put on his little-boy-lost expression. 'That's a pity because Francesca will be so disappointed if you don't come.'

In spite of herself she couldn't help smiling. 'When you use that wheedling tone of voice, Max, you think you can twist me round your little finger, don't you?'

And he was dead right, too. She was weakening by the second.

He put both hands on her arms and smiled down at her.

For one breathtaking moment she thought he was going to kiss her, right there in the corridor!

'I'll drive you over this evening. Bring your toothbrush, Tessa.'

She bridled. 'Max, I don't think…'

He dropped his hands from her arms as the rakish grin spread over his face. 'What I mean is, you don't want to have to drink lemonade all evening simply because you've got to drive back to hospital, do you? And the pink bedroom is still waiting for someone to sleep in it.'

'The pink bedroom looked very cosy,' she conceded, with a shy smile. 'Maybe I'll take you up on it.'

He looked pleased. 'I thought you might.'

As she turned away she thought how maddeningly sure of himself he was. Where she was concerned he thought he simply had to crook his little finger and she'd resume their affair.

She groaned inwardly. Even though she wanted more commitment than Max would ever be prepared to give, she knew she wanted him desperately. But on any terms?

She'd think about that later when she had more time. Better not to dwell too much on the problem when she had a busy day ahead of her.

She ate a piece of toast and drank coffee in the medical staff dining room, before hurrying up to the ward. Pushing open the swing doors, she reflected that she'd try really hard to make herself sleep in the pink bedroom tonight. But if, by any chance…

'Am I glad to see you, Sister!'

Staff Nurse Anne Reeves seemed uncharacteristically excited about something.

'What's happened?'

Tessa glanced down the ward. Everything seemed orga-

nised and her nurses were going about their duties in a con-
trolled, calm manner.

'It's Helen Cooper and Becky Grayson. They've both
gone into labour and—'

'Well, they're both near enough to full term. Becky's
blood pressure was normal yesterday and Helen's latest scan
showed a remarkable repositioning of the placenta. Thanks
to the bed rest and medication, there's been no bleeding for
weeks. She requested a normal birth rather than a Caesarean.
Max has agreed, providing there are no further complications, so—'

'Yes, but that's not all. Guess what? They were chatting
together early this morning and they discovered that—'

'I know what you're going to say!'

Tessa clamped a hand over her mouth as she remembered
the coincidence she'd suspected when Becky had come in
and had explained that she'd been born at Moortown
General and adopted soon after her birth.

'Helen told me the whole story when I arrived on duty,'
Anne went on, still in the same excited manner. 'She told
me that you knew about her having to give up her first baby
for adoption. Anyway, when her waters broke this morning
she started crying. Becky was trying to comfort her and
Helen just started telling her about this lovely baby girl,
born in this hospital and given up for adoption twenty-two
years ago.'

Tessa, although having originally suspected there might
be a happy coincidence in the two women having been
brought together, felt stunned.

'And I suppose Becky opened up and told her she'd—'

'Yes, they quickly put two and two together. Helen was
a bit confused about the name. She said she'd called her
baby Susan, but Becky explained that her adoptive mother

had told her, just before she died, that her name at birth had been Susan.'

'So, are they both convinced that…?'

'Oh, the most convincing piece of evidence, as they say in the TV dramas, was a cloth rabbit,' Anne said, her face wreathed in smiles.

Tessa was confused. 'A cloth rabbit?'

Anne nodded. 'Yes. Apparently, Helen had made a cloth rabbit while she was in hospital, expecting her first baby. She gave it to the baby girl when she was born. This cloth rabbit was the only thing that the baby was allowed to keep when she was adopted.'

'And Becky…?'

'Becky said the cloth rabbit was her most treasured possession. She'd brought it with her into hospital to give to her own baby. When she took this battered old rabbit out of her bedside cupboard and showed it to Helen they both started crying, as you can imagine.'

Tessa gave herself a little shake. The meeting of mother and long lost daughter, exciting though it was, would have to take second place to the delivery of their respective babies.

She removed her cuffs and rolled up her sleeves above the elbow. 'Well, let's get these babies delivered, Anne.'

She found Helen lying on her back, taking deep breaths as she stared up at the ceiling. She gave Tessa a tired smile as she approached the bed.

'They've just taken Becky to the delivery room, Sister. Her pains are coming quicker than mine now but— Ooh…that's another one. I'm speeding up. Becky was timing me but— Ooh…'

Tessa swished the curtains round the bed and pulled back the covers. A swift examination revealed that the top of the birth canal was opening up to prepare for the baby's expulsion from the womb.

'I'll take you on to the delivery room, Helen. Shouldn't be long now,' Tessa said briskly. 'Your baby's in a good position so just try to relax. I'll give you something to ease the contractions when we get into the delivery room.'

Helen held onto Tessa's hand as the porter wheeled her down the ward, through the swing doors and into the delivery suite.

Max was just coming out of one of the rooms, wiping his hands on a dressing sheet, a happy expression on his face.

'Another satisfied customer,' he told Tessa. 'A little boy for Becky. Talk about a precipitous birth! We barely had time to get her on the table when the little fellow shot out like greased lightning. She's over the moon!'

On the trolley Helen attempted to sit up, only to be forced back by another contraction.

'Pant, Helen,' Tessa urged, holding tightly to her patient's hand.

Helen stopped panting as the contraction eased and looked up at Tessa.

'I never thought I'd be a grandmother before I'd be a proper mother,' she said, her eyes shining with happiness. 'Just think, thirty-seven and a grandmother! Is that a record, do you think?'

Max looked puzzled. 'What is Helen—?'

'Ooh, Sister…!'

Helen clutched more tightly at Tessa's hand as a particularly strong contraction swept over her.

With the help of one of the midwives, Max lifted her onto the delivery table. Tessa reached for the entonox machine and instructed Helen how to breath into the mask to relieve the pain.

'Not long now, Helen,' she said as she wiped her patient's forehead with a soothing lotion.

Max was concentrating on manoeuvring the baby's head into the correct position. Briefly, he looked up to tell Tessa that there was no problem with the placenta. She was relieved to hear it. Although Helen had made excellent progress during the final weeks of her pregnancy, Tessa had still felt some anxiety when Max had agreed to a normal birth.

He was easing out the shoulders. After that it was only seconds before Helen's baby was in his hands and wailing lustily.

'You've got a little girl, Helen,' Max said gently.

Tessa swallowed hard as she watched the happy mother's face crease up until she was sobbing joyfully almost as loudly as her new daughter was wailing.

Tessa wiped Helen's eyes with a tissue. 'Would you like to hold her?'

There were more tears as Helen took hold of her little girl, carefully checking each tiny toe, each small finger.

'She's perfect, just like my Susan was.'

'So, what will you call your new daughter?' Tessa asked.

Helen hesitated. 'Well, I was going to call her Susan, but I've got the real Susan back now so I don't need a substitute. I'm going to call her Rosemary after my mother.'

She leaned back against her pillows, cradling her baby with one arm as she ran a hand through her damp grey and auburn hair.

'Rosemary,' she repeated happily. 'You know, Sister, just before my mum died she told me she wished she'd let me keep my baby. She regretted not bringing Susan up as her own. So she'd be really thrilled to know I've not only got Susan back but I've also got a new baby and a grandson.'

One of the staff midwives came in to tell Tessa that the

two new fathers had just arrived. Mr Cooper and Mr Grayson were anxious to see their wives and babies.

'That's my Graham and Becky's Victor,' Helen said. 'Did you phone them, Sister?'

Tessa nodded. 'We tried to get them here on time to be with you but…'

'I think Graham will be relieved to have missed the birth,' Helen said wryly, 'but he'll be dying to see the baby. And I've got a lot of explaining to do. I'd told him about Susan but he's going to be stunned when I explain…'

She stopped and grabbed Tessa's hand.

'Sister, will you stay with me in case he faints or anything when I tell him I've got my first daughter back and she's had a little boy so he's now a step-grandfather as well?'

'Of course I will!'

'What was Helen talking about?' Max asked, as he followed Tessa into her office later that morning.

She picked up the half-full cafetière. Anne must have taken her coffee-break earlier. Good! With any luck they wouldn't be interrupted.

'I haven't had a minute to explain, Max,' she said, as she poured out a couple of cups.

He sank down into one of the squashy armchairs. 'Well, don't keep me in suspense.'

She smiled as she briefly outlined the incredible turn of events.

'They'll have to check out the formalities of the situation with the authorities but that ancient little cloth rabbit has convinced me.'

His eyes widened with surprise. 'I would never have made the connection, would you?'

'I must admit it crossed my mind but I thought it unlikely. Becky had spent her childhood in Australia, but it turns out her adoptive parents emigrated there when she was tiny. She wasn't called Susan any more but adoptive parents often change the names of their babies, especially when they take them very young.'

'If we'd had Helen's records from twenty-two years ago it would have triggered our suspicions, I suppose,' Max said. 'Any more coffee?'

'I can squeeze a drop for a thirsty worker.' She tipped up the cafetière. 'Want me to make some more?'

'Haven't time.'

He drained his cup and placed it on the table, before putting both hands on the sides of her arms and leaning towards her with an earnest expression.

'Six o'clock in the car park. OK?'

She gave him a wry smile. 'You know it's OK. I wouldn't let Francesca down on her sixteenth birthday.'

For the second time that morning she thought he was going to kiss her. His head was inclined towards her but he simply smiled, a secretive sort of smile, hinting that he was hoping for more than a mere kiss when they next got together.

She gave a deep sigh as the door closed behind him. What strategy should she use tonight? How could she convince him that she didn't want an affair, that love and commitment went together, that sooner or later he was going to have to remove the emotional shell he'd built around himself?

He knew how to function on a physical level. Function was an understatement when describing the wonderful experience they'd shared when they'd made love. But was it possible to live life on a purely physical level?

Max seemed to think so. She knew that because he'd been hurt so badly this was his subconscious way of dealing with his emotions. He had no intention of ever being hurt again so therefore he resisted becoming too involved.

She stood up, rinsed the cups under the tap, dried her hands and put her cuffs back on her sleeves. She would go down to the postnatal section and check on the new arrivals. Immersing herself in work, it would soon stop her worrying about her own problems.

Becky and Helen had been moved into the same unit, side by side, the two cots between their beds.

Becky, her unruly golden hair cascading around her shoulders, was feeding her tiny son. She smiled when Tessa approached.

Tessa perched on the side of her bed. 'How's baby Tim?'

'I think he's lived on this earth before. He knew exactly how to feed without me explaining a thing. Just like his Aunty Rosemary over there.'

Tessa laughed as she turned to look at Helen who was rubbing her new baby's back as she waited for the post-feed burps.

'Rosemary looks very young to be an aunty,' Tessa said. 'How are you feeling, Helen?'

Helen smiled happily. 'Fine.'

'And you, Becky?'

'It was like shelling peas. Timmy couldn't wait to get here.' She smiled. 'Helen and I haven't stopped talking since we got back.'

'We've got a lot of catching up to do,' Helen said fondly.

'Plenty of time, Mum,' Becky said. 'Can I call you Mum?'

'I'll be very cross if you don't, my girl,' Helen said, with mock severity. 'Do you know, Sister, my hair used to be the same colour as Becky's. Can you imagine that?'

'Absolutely!' Tessa said, looking at the faded auburn strands mingling with the grey on Helen's head.

'I'm glad you've kept your hair long, Becky,' Helen said.

'But if you've got a hairbrush handy it could do with a bit of a—'

Becky grinned. 'Oh, Mum! I've been too busy to do my hair this morning, haven't I?'

'Tell you what,' Tessa put in quickly. 'I'll ask the hairdresser to come in and give you both a shampoo and blow-dry.'

'So, mother and daughter are getting on really well, are they?' Max said, as he placed a vase of fresh roses on the kitchen table.

Tessa smiled. 'Like a house on fire.'

'It's an incredible story,' Francesca said. 'Don't you think you should phone the *Moortown Echo*?'

Max pulled a wry face. 'And have the place swarming with reporters? No, we'll leave it to Helen and Becky. If they want publicity they can get it when they go home.'

'Lovely roses, Dad. Did you get those because it's my birthday?'

Max's face was deep in concentration as he removed the gold paper from a bottle of champagne, unwired the cork and proceeded to aid it to leave the neck.

'I always think opening a champagne bottle is like delivering a baby. You mustn't pull it out too quickly. In fact, you mustn't pull it at all. It's got to slip out in its own good time while you gently ease…'

There was an explosive pop and the cork shot out in a froth of bubbles.

Tessa grabbed a glass and placed it in a strategic place where Max could begin pouring.

'Frisky little brew, this one.'

Tessa laughed. 'Good thing your babies didn't emerge like that today, Max.'

'How many babies did you deliver today, Dad?'

Max took a sip of champagne. 'Lost count,' he said airily. 'Dozens!'

Francesca's eyes widened. 'No kidding!'

'Well…four actually!'

'Oh, Dad!'

As Tessa looked across at Max she felt a surge of un-welcome emotion. Unwelcome because she didn't know how to deal with it. How was she to quell this wonderful feeling of belonging, of being an integral part of this family, when she was only a…

She took another sip of champagne. It seemed to be going straight to her head. She'd had a tiring day and she'd skipped lunch to do some shopping.

She was only a casual visitor in this family, she told her-self firmly. Like Max, if she was to survive she mustn't get too involved.

But there was such a warm atmosphere tonight. It was difficult not to be swept along and forget the transience of her situation.

Her heart was telling her to go with the flow, whereas her head was instructing her to hold back. The champagne was definitely going to her head! Perhaps she could take the least line of resistance…just this once…

Max produced a superb birthday supper.

'Thanks, Dad,' Francesca said, as she polished off her second helping of profiteroles and cream. 'All my favourite food tonight.'

'Courtesy of Marks and Spencer,' Max said, with a wry grin. 'I've been too busy to cook this week so I asked one of the nurses to collect all this when she went out at lunch-time.'

'The chicken Kiev was delicious,' Tessa said, feeling an unwelcome pang of something akin to jealousy as she wondered which of the many nurses who drooled after Max had obliged with the shopping.

'You can come to my real party on Saturday if you'd like to, Tessa. Dad's not coming till the end to collect me but—'

'That's awfully sweet of you, Francesca, but I think I'm on duty,' Tessa said quickly.

Max smiled. 'What Tessa means is that teenage discos aren't her scene any more.'

'You're not too old, Tessa!' Francesca said. 'I mean, Dad's forty so...'

'Well, thank you very much,' Max said, with mock indignation. 'I'm not yet over the hill. I can still beat you at tennis, my girl.'

He turned to Tessa. 'I've been having the old tennis court at the bottom of the garden resurfaced. You'll have to come over for a game when it's finished.'

'Dad's fantastic at tennis,' Francesca said. 'At our club in the States he used to beat everybody—including me. But I've got youth on my side so sooner or later I'm going to get my own back. So will you come over during the summer, Tessa?'

'I'll try when I'm not working.'

'You work too hard,' Max said, his tone softening.

Francesca pushed back her chair. 'Got to finish my homework. Birthday or no birthday, they don't let you off the hook at my school. Thanks again for the fabulous present, Tessa.'

Tessa smiled. 'Glad you liked it.'

She'd decided this morning that the book she'd bought for Francesca was a bit of a dull present so she'd raced out to the shops. It hadn't been easy to think of what to buy for a very special sixteen-year-old but in the end she'd lashed out on a pair of silk pyjamas from the boutique where she and Max had bought the cashmere sweater.

And while she'd been there she'd just happened to indulge herself with some lacy lingerie. Why she'd put it on tonight she simply couldn't imagine! But she'd tried to convince herself it was because her own stack of serviceable bras and panties had reached an all-time low of drab grey.

'I'm not going to offer to help with the dishwasher, Max,' Tessa said, as the kitchen door closed behind Francesca. 'I've seen how efficient you are on the domestic front and I'd probably put things in the wrong place.'

He gave her a languid, heart-rending smile. 'That's a good excuse, but I'll let you off, knowing you've had a hard day. Let's take our coffee through into the sitting room. Would you like a brandy—just a small one to celebrate Francesca's birthday?'

She shook her head. 'I'm feeling decidedly woozy with the champagne. Got to keep a clear head.'

He put an arm round her waist and guided her through the door.

'Why? So you can analyse why I want to make love to you tonight?'

'Max!'

She glanced up the stairs towards the first landing where Francesca would, hopefully, be ensconced in her room.

He gave her a rakish grin as he propelled her into the sitting room and closed the door. As soon as they were inside he swung round and took her in his arms.

'Don't worry about Francesca. She adores you and she's not a child any more. Think back to when you were sixteen. That was only two years before you enrolled as a student nurse and had to face all sorts of life-and-death situations.'

'I know she's nearly grown up but…Max, how does she feel about her father making love to…?'

She stopped, unable to continue as Max propelled her

towards the sofa. He settled her back against the cushions and pulled her close against him.

'I'm sure she doesn't mind,' he said gently. 'Especially if it's somebody like you.'

'But how does she know I'm not going to turn out like Vanessa and Carol?'

She heard the expulsion of his breath as his arm tightened around her.

'Because you're in a quite different category. I was a fool to get involved with Vanessa and then, not having learned my lesson, I got involved with Carol. But I was missing Catherine—oh, yes, I missed her, Tessa. I couldn't forget all the good times we'd had together. For me, our marriage only turned sour on that final day. Before that...'

She held her breath as he paused, not wanting to break up his train of thought.

'Before that it had been wonderful. So, because I'm a normal man with a normal sexual need, I deliberately looked for a good-time girl. Someone to have a purely sexual relationship with. Someone who wouldn't want me to fall in love and...'

'And commit yourself to them?'

'Exactly. But it didn't work that way. Vanessa started talking weddings. I let her down as easily as I could. She couldn't have been too devastated because she married someone else six months later. I think she was in love with the idea of being married.'

'How about Carol?'

He ran a hand through his hair. 'Carol was a mistake from the start. She was a very sexy lady. She practically threw herself at me and I simply couldn't resist her physical advances. She fulfilled a physical need for a few weeks before I realised she was getting on my nerves.'

'So you gave her the chop?'

He nodded. 'I think that was when I realised that purely physical relationships don't work.'

'I could have told you that without having the trauma of going through the wounding experiences,' she said quietly.

'But you weren't around when all this was happening. If you'd been there…'

She waited with bated breath.

'But you weren't… Anyway, that was when I decided I wouldn't have any more meaningless physical relationships. I made sure that I wasn't giving out any signals that might give the wrong impression. When you're single people automatically assume you're on the lookout for another partner.'

'What about meaningful relationships?' she asked quietly.

He turned towards her and gave a long, slow smile. 'Those are the only ones that matter. But they can be difficult to handle. Especially if you pick a spirited, self opinionated, impossibly demanding…'

His lips closed over hers and she didn't resist the steady, throbbing magic of his kiss. She revelled in the waves of insistent passion that were sweeping over her.

'Tessa, you will stay with me tonight, won't you?' he whispered, his voice huskily sensuous.

She knew she couldn't resist him. She was in too deep. But he'd made it clear that she was different from his other girlfriends, hadn't he? Did that mean that his ideas of relationships were changing, that he was actually thinking about committing himself…possibly in some dim and distant future?

She gave a slight inclination of her head, answering his question in a barely audible voice. 'I'll stay.'

She knew that if she slept with Max tonight she would be involving herself too deeply to go back. She never did things by halves. She wouldn't want to end their relationship.

Only Max might want to do that. But she was willing to take a chance.

He kissed her slowly, tenderly, with only a hint of the passion that she sensed was already roused. He was holding himself off, saving himself for their night together.

When he went into the kitchen to finish clearing up she remained on the sofa, staring into the dying embers of the fire, making a valiant effort to convince herself that she wasn't mad. She gave an involuntary shiver as she remembered the first night she'd spent with Max and she knew that once she was in his arms again all her doubts would vanish.

He returned from the kitchen and switched on the CD player. She chose Rachmaninov's second piano concerto from the CDs he offered her and lay back against his arm, closing her eyes as the haunting melodies flowed over her.

'I love the poignancy of the middle movement,' Max said, his arm tightening around her shoulders.

She opened her eyes and looked at his handsome profile outlined in the flickering firelight. Max had deliberately left open the long, heavy, curtains so that they could see the sky as it turned from red sunset through pink and gold to a grey darkness, lit only by a pale crescent moon.

'So do I,' she whispered, glad to find that in spite of his efforts to hide it deep down Max was a true romantic.

When Francesca called down to say she was going to go to sleep, Max put the fireguard round the dying embers and took hold of Tessa's hand.

Together they said goodnight to Francesca. She didn't try to detain them. Tessa had the distinct impression she was being decidedly tactful this evening.

Max led her down the landing to his room. He closed the door, locking it on the inside.

She breathed a sigh of relief. 'I'm glad you did that. I wouldn't want Francesca to come in when—'

'She wouldn't do that. She's grown up enough to know we have a right to our privacy. But, knowing how sensitive you are, I locked it anyway.'

He pulled her into his arms. Her senses began to rouse as gently, oh, so gently he started to undress her.

By the time the expensive, flimsy underwear had been cast into a heap on top of her jeans and sweater she was impatiently unbuttoning his shirt, her urgent desire for fulfilment making her completely abandoned.

The bed was turned back, the sheets cool and inviting as he pulled her against him. They dispensed with all but the briefest preliminaries, both of them desperate to reach fulfilment.

Some time later, he was ready to take her again, this time more slowly, savouring each delicate caress, each tantalising movement of their entwined bodies, until she had to hold herself back from screaming out loud with ecstasy…

When she heard the noise of the house martins she knew immediately where she was. Opening her eyes, she padded, naked, over the carpet to look out of the window. For a few moments she watched the mother bird feeding her young, their tiny, fluffy heads peeping out of the mud nest that had been built under the eaves.

Turning back, she saw that Max was now awake and watching her, shielding the morning sun from his eyes with one hand.

'The eggs have hatched, Max. They've got babies now.'

'That's why they're making so much noise. Come back to bed.' He patted the sheet beside him.

'Shouldn't we be making a move?' She glanced at the clock. 'Francesca will be bringing the tea. I'd better—'

He laughed. 'Oh, don't start that charade again. She would have brought mine already if she'd thought I was on my own. Why don't you accept that you've been accepted...as part of the family.'

He'd tossed out the remark so casually. Did he know how much it meant to her?

Slowly she retraced her steps over the carpet.

'Well, are you coming back or do I have to come and get you?'

She shrieked with laughter as he sprang out of bed and lunged for her, pulling her back into the warmth of the bed and the impossibly tantalising embrace of his arms...

CHAPTER EIGHT

STANDING at the opposite side of the delivery table from Max, Tessa reflected that it was exactly a week since Francesca's birthday evening. That had been the turning point. That had been the idyllic night when she'd realised that she wanted to be with Max on any terms.

It had been a conscious decision, in many ways a scary one, committing herself to an unknown future. But she'd told herself that life was unpredictable anyway. You never knew what was round the corner. All the usual clichés had flown through her head as she'd lain in his arms, listening to the sound of the house martins feeding their young.

Max had been so solicitous with her that morning, seemingly reluctant to return to their real world of work. They'd laughed and joked together in Max's huge bath like a couple of children. But when it was all over they'd had to return and become professional people in their caring profession.

She bent down to wipe her patient's forehead with a soft piece of gauze. Jill Mason's face was puckered again as a strong contraction began to force itself upon her.

'You can start to push with this one, Jill,' Max said. 'The first baby's head is peeping out now.'

Tessa squeezed her patient's hand, admiring her stoical bravery. Jill had chosen to have a normal delivery for her twins so that her sister, Samantha, could be at the bedside to watch their arrival and bond with them immediately as her own. Tessa glanced at Samantha who was now leaning forward over the table, almost touching Max's arms as he manoeuvred the head into position.

144

'Oh, Jill, you should just see his little head!' Samantha said excitedly.

But Jill, her face screwed up with the pain of the next contraction, was oblivious to everything as she concentrated on the final stage of her delivery.

As the baby boy arrived in Max's hands, Samantha was already reaching out to take him.

'Oh, please, Doctor, let me just touch him… Ooh, he's all slippery! Jill, he's wonderful. So small and so perfect!'

'Tessa,' Max said quickly. 'Take charge of this little one. The other one's on his way.'

The second baby was fully delivered barely ten minutes later, by which time Tessa had cleansed the first baby's tiny nostrils, ensured that he was breathing properly, wrapped him in a warm dressing sheet and handed him to the ecstatic Samantha.

She dealt with the second baby boy in the same way. Samantha beamed happily as he, too, was placed in her other arm. Jill, meanwhile, lay back against the pillow, trying to catch her breath.

Tessa wiped a soothing lotion over Jill's face, before drying her off with a soft piece of gauze.

Two of the staff midwives were trying to persuade Samantha to relinquish the babies for a little while so that they could weigh them and carry out the routine postnatal checks.

Samantha, still in a state of euphoria, moved to sit on the chair beside her sister.

'You were brilliant, Sis,' she said quietly. 'How are you feeling?'

Jill gave a wry grin. 'Like I've been tossed around in a tumble dryer…but I feel a lot lighter! Think I might go swimming this afternoon.'

Samantha grinned. 'We'll all go down to the river. We'll teach the twins to do the breaststroke and—'

'The twins will be in incubators for a few days,' one of the midwives, unused to the make-believe, nonsensical chatter of the sisters, said quickly.

Samantha's jocular manner changed instantly. 'Why? What's wrong with them?'

'There's nothing wrong with them,' Tessa said, 'apart from being slightly underweight. We'd expected this because Jill was only eight months when they were delivered.'

Max, having supervised the transference of the babies into incubators, came across the room. 'As soon as your twins reach five pounds, Samantha, you can take them home.'

He turned to look at Tessa and said quietly, 'Let's take a break while it's quiet.'

Walking beside him through the swing doors and back down the ward to her office, she experienced a warm glow of togetherness. She was well aware that the grapevine had started buzzing with speculation about her relationship with Max. Everyone seemed to think they were speeding in the direction of wedding bells.

If only!

Max was holding open the door to her office. She smiled up at him as she walked through. He was looking decidedly carefree at the moment.

Hannah had told her, during a pause in one of their afternoon clinics, that this was one of the things that her fellow medical staff were remarking on—the transformation from dour, uncommunicative, forty-something consultant to Max's present, easygoing, almost boyish demeanour.

Tessa poured boiling water onto the coffee grounds as she reflected that it was easy for her colleagues to speculate about the state of her relationship with Max. It was good;

it was fantastic when they were together! But how long would it last?

She pushed forcefully down on the metal rod in the middle of the cafetière.

'The tennis court's ready for play,' Max said, as she handed him a cup. 'Are you free this weekend?'

She hesitated. 'I could be.'

He smiled. 'What's that supposed to mean?'

'I haven't finalised the weekend duty roster yet. I need to leave a reliable, experienced staff nurse in charge of the ward. Anne Reeves has asked for some time with her fiancé so—'

'Anne's always having time off to be with her fiancé.'

'Well, the wedding's coming up soon and—'

'They've got a whole lifetime to be together,' Max interrupted. 'Whereas we…'

'Go on,' she prompted.

He put down his cup and faced her. 'Whereas we only get a little time together when we're not working.'

She forced herself not to make a sharp retort. She wanted so desperately to point out that it was Max's fault that their relationship was so transitory.

'Tell you what,' she said slowly. 'I'll split the off-duty time with Anne. I'll work Saturday and take Sunday off. Anne can have Saturday off. She's got to help her bridesmaids with a dress fitting.'

'So, if you're free on Sunday, you could come over after duty on Saturday and spend the night with me.'

'I'm going home Saturday night,' she said, quickly, feeling the need to assert herself. 'I'll come over on Sunday afternoon.'

If she played hard to get it might make Max see she had a life of her own, and that she wasn't always available at his beck and call. And if she kept her own family life going, it would soften the blow for her if or when Max decided he'd tired of their liaison.

She saw an enigmatic expression flit across his face, a relic of the old Max before he'd started opening up towards her.

'OK,' he said quietly. 'If it's so important for you to go home this weekend, I'll—'

'Max, it's important for me to keep contact with my family.'

She nearly added that they were the only family she'd got and she'd need them badly to help her pick up the pieces if Max disappeared from her life. But she held her tongue. The last time she'd asked where their relationship was going she thought he'd gone off her permanently!

Waking up in her own room at home on a Sunday morning was always pleasant. Entirely different to how she would have wakened if she'd spent the night with Max over in Cragdale. But this was a tactical move!

She visualised him lying in bed now, his dark, tousled hair falling over his forehead, maybe his hands clasped behind his head as he lay back amongst the pillows, listening to the house martins. Was he missing her? She certainly hoped so, otherwise her tactics would have been wasted.

He didn't seem to be tiring of their relationship. Far from it! He was always coming up with some new idea to fill their off-duty time together.

The summer was going to be wonderful, with all the plans he was making. Tennis, swimming in the Cragdale river, open-air concerts and long walks were only some of the ideas he'd outlined for what looked like being an exciting few weeks.

But there had been no talk of the autumn or the winter.

When the days became shorter again and the chill wind blew over the moors, would that signal the end of their idyll?

Someone was tapping on her bedroom door. She raised herself on her pillows to see her sister-in-law coming in with a mug of tea.

'Breakfast's nearly ready, Tessa,' Gemma said, putting the mug down on her bedside table. 'Must dash. The kids are helping your mum set the table and it's chaos down there in the kitchen.'

'Thanks a lot for the tea, Gemma.'

Before the door closed, the appetising aroma of bacon and eggs had wafted up the stairs into her room. She took a sip of her tea, before leaping out of bed.

Better get down there to help Mum.

It was decided over breakfast that Tessa should stay home and look after Felicity and Michael so that the rest of the family could go to church that morning.

'You're sure you don't mind, Tessa?' her brother asked. 'On your day off, I mean. Sounds like a busman's holiday to me.'

Tessa assured Richard she would enjoy having the children all to herself. 'It was my idea, wasn't it?'

'She'll make somebody a good wife,' Fred said.

Their invaluable farm worker always came in for breakfast with the family after he'd fed the hens and milked the few cows that remained from the large, magnificent herd her father had reared.

Fred had been working on the farm ever since Tessa could remember and he didn't seem to have changed. She figured that he must have looked older than his years when she was a child.

In those far-off days she'd had the impression he was a tall man, but actually he was barely as tall as she was now and his rounded shoulders were making him shrink even more.

'He'll be a lucky man that gets our Tessa.'

Fred was in full conversational flow now. 'Mark my words…'

'More tea, Fred,' Tessa said quickly, picking up the big brown, earthenware teapot.

'Don't mind if I do, lass. Now, where was I? Oh, yes…'

'How's that nice doctor you brought over here that day when you walked over the moors?' her mother began, interrupting the flow of Fred's meanderings.

Trust her mother to be as subtle as a sledgehammer!

'He's fine,' Tessa said. 'Isn't it time you were all getting ready for church? You're going to be late.'

'Plenty of time,' her mother said calmly. She leaned forward, her shrewd eyes narrowing as she looked at Tessa. 'Are you still seeing him?'

'We work together, Mum.'

'I know that. What I mean is, do you go out together when you're off duty?'

Tessa could feel the beginning of a tell-tale flush spreading over her cheeks.

'Occasionally,' she answered vaguely. 'I'll start clearing up.'

She was already on her feet when her mother dropped her bombshell.

'Why don't you ask him to lunch today? That leg of lamb is enormous and we always cook too many vegetables.'

'Yes, why don't you?' her brother asked, a knowing twinkle in his eye. 'Get on the phone now before he goes out.'

'He's probably on duty.'

'I thought Mum told me he was a consultant. They never work on Sundays if they can help it,' Richard said.

It was a conspiracy! They were all dying to get her 'fixed

up with a young man', as Fred would put it. She bowed to
pressure but insisted on going upstairs to make the call to
Max. She wasn't going to treat them all to hearing her conversation on the kitchen phone.

Max seemed surprised at her invitation but jumped at the
chance to enjoy a real Sunday roast on the farm.

'Francesca's spending the weekend at a friend's house in
Moortown,' he said, 'So I probably wouldn't have got round
to making lunch.'

She felt a moment of panic at the thought of the third-
degree interrogation he might be submitted to around the
lunch table.

'I can say you're working if you'd find it an ordeal,' she
said quickly.

'Why should I find it an ordeal?'

'I think they've all got the wrong idea,' she said cau-
tiously. 'They think we might be…well, more than we are,
if you know what I mean.'

There was a pause before he replied. 'Oh, let them think
what they like. I'm not turning down a good lunch. I can
field their questions.'

As she put down the phone she reflected that Max would
give a good account of himself. He was used to having to
be diplomatic with patients and their relatives. He never
gave away any more than he had to.

In any situation!

'I remember your husband very well, Mrs Grainger,' Max
said affably, as Tessa's mother helped him to a second helping of roast potatoes.

The conversation at the table had centred on Tessa's father for the last few minutes, her mother reminiscing at
some length about the good old days when there used to be
four farm workers with their wives and children and all her

own family at Sunday lunch. She'd explained how there had been trestle tables all down the side of the kitchen.

'That's how I found my babysitter here,' Max continued, turning to smile at Tessa. 'I was asking around the club-house and Mr Grainger spoke about his daughter in glowing terms.'

She smiled back, feeling a surge of unwanted pride that he was being so well accepted by her family. She knew she had no right to be proud of him. He was totally independent of her.

All the same, she basked in his reflected glory. It was going to be so difficult to explain to her mother that they were just good friends. She was sure she wouldn't believe her. Hawk-eyed as always, her mother hadn't taken her eyes off the pair of them!

Max had a second helping of apple pie and custard. Tessa whispered to him that he'd never be able to cope with their game of tennis that afternoon. He whispered back that they could always change their plans and rest for a while be-forehand.

They stayed on long enough to have coffee in the sitting room, but Tessa was aware that Max kept glancing at his watch. It certainly wasn't the ordeal that she'd half expected but neither of them could relax with the family obviously trying to assess their relationship.

Max put down his cup and stood up, smiling around the room. 'I promised Tessa a game of tennis this afternoon. Thank you so much, Mrs Grainger, for the excellent lunch.'

As Tessa's mother accompanied them to the door she was assuring Max that he was welcome to come and see them any time. Max picked up Tessa's weekend bag and carried it out to the car. The children, playing on the swing in the garden, waved goodbye.

'You didn't tell me a story,' Michael called.

'Next time I will,' Max shouted back.

So there was going to be a next time!

'That wasn't too difficult, was it?' she asked, as the car moved away up the cobbled track towards the main road.

'You've got a lovely family,' Max said, adjusting the rear-view mirror so that he could take a last look at the farm and the waving children, now clustered around their grandmother.

'Everybody's so warm-hearted. It must have been wonderful, growing up in a family like that.'

'I suppose it was,' she said slowly. 'I've never really thought about it—always took it for granted.'

'You should never take anything for granted.'

His voice was suddenly serious. 'I never do…nowadays.'

He drove on in silence, his eyes steadfastly on the road as they climbed out of Riversdale and crossed the stretch of moor that led to Cragdale.

She couldn't begin to imagine what he'd meant by that remark. She closed her eyes and leaned back against the headrest of the passenger seat. Better to let it pass. Max didn't like to be analysed!

He beat her at tennis. They played three sets and he won them all. Exhausted though she was at the end of the afternoon, she had to admit it had been great fun. Max was a very good player but winning the game wasn't the be-all and end-all for him. He played in a relaxed manner that gave them time to talk to each other in between shots.

'I'll beat you next time,' she joked, rubbing a towel over her face. The remains of her make-up had evaporated in the heat of the afternoon sun.

'You played a good game, Tessa,' he called from the

middle of the court, where he was lowering the net and looping it over itself. 'Come on, I'll make you some tea.'

'You've got youth on your side,' he told her with a wry grin a few minutes later as they sat at the kitchen table, waiting for the tea in the blue and white willow-pattern teapot to brew. 'One day you'll probably beat me.'

She held her breath. 'One day,' she repeated, watching his reaction. 'You mean in the dim and distant future.'

He hesitated. 'You're ten years younger than me. That makes a big difference when you reach a certain age.'

'Oh, you poor old thing!'

She tried to turn it into a joke when what she really wanted to do was ask if he thought they'd still be together in those later years he was referring to. He'd obviously given it some thought so there was a glimmer of hope.

Hope! That was all she had to cling to because it was no good trying to force his hand.

There was the sound of a car in the drive.

'That will be Francesca's friend's parents, bringing her back.'

He stood up. Tessa heard the sound of the car stopping but driving away almost immediately.

'I'm home!'

Francesca was calling from the hallway. Her footsteps could be heard along the corridor and then she burst into the kitchen, her face wreathed in smiles.

'Had a fantastic time. They've got a swimming pool in their garden. Oh, hi, Tessa!'

She flung her canvas bag onto a chair and joined them at the table.

'Why don't we make a swimming pool, Dad? There's plenty of room at the bottom of the garden.'

'Because I'm only renting this place. The owners were

delighted when I said I'd do up their old tennis court at my own expense, but I don't want to spend a vast amount of money on putting in a pool if...'

He stopped in mid-sentence, looking first at Francesca and then at Tessa.

'If what, Dad?'

'Well, if we have to move somewhere else.'

A cold hand seemed to clutch at Tessa's heart.

'But we don't want to move, do we, Tessa?' Francesca said, forcefully.

'It's got nothing to do with me,' Tessa said quickly. 'I'm not involved in this.'

'Yes, you are,' Francesca persisted. 'You like being here with Dad, don't you? We've got the option to buy this place so why don't we?'

'Francesca!' Max put his hand on his daughter's arm to quell the flow of words. 'Can we leave this discussion to another time?'

Francesca started breathing heavily but remained silent. Tessa leaned back in her chair, avoiding Max's eyes.

'Did you manage to do any homework while you were at Joanna's?' he was asking his daughter.

Francesca turned a mutinous expression towards her father. 'Didn't have time. I'll go and get on with it now.'

She paused at the kitchen door. 'Are you staying for supper, Tessa?'

'I have to get back to the hospital,' Tessa said, standing up.

'Well, see you soon, I hope.' Francesca closed the door.

'What's the rush?' Max said, coming round the table to look down at her with a quizzical expression.

'I promised Anne I'd get back to the ward for the last couple of hours so she could have the remains of Sunday evening with her fiancé.'

He raised an eyebrow. 'That was very noble of you. Very much over and beyond the call of duty. So Anne's fiancé gains and I have to…'

'Oh, I'm sure you'll find something to do,' she said in an easy tone. 'I'm not the only pebble on the beach.'

It was an unfortunate turn of phrase. As soon as she'd said it she wished she hadn't. She didn't want Max trawling through his address book for phone numbers of possible substitutes.

It was a very difficult path she was treading. She only hoped her tactics were working.

He walked with her to the door and out to her car, kissing her gently on the lips before she drove away. Looking back in the rear-mirror, she could see he was still standing in the drive watching her disappear.

She gave a big sigh, longing to turn the car around and drive straight back. Restricting their time together like this had better be worth the awful feeling of deprivation that was sweeping over her.

Some time in the future would she look back and think, yes, that was how I won Max round? Or would she remember him only as a friend who passed briefly through her life?

Only time would tell.

'So, how's the romance going?' Hannah said, as Tessa started to reset the examination trolley in their afternoon obstetrics clinic.

'It's going…but I don't know in which direction,' Tessa said, clattering a couple of kidney dishes down onto a sterile dressing sheet.

'You mean Max isn't ready to commit himself yet?' Hannah asked shrewdly.

'Something like that.' Tessa turned her attention to the

examination couch, removing the used sheet and replacing it with a clean one.

'It's early days, Tessa,' Hannah said in a soothing voice. 'So long as you're enjoying life together he'll realise he can't live without you.'

Tessa swung round to face her. 'What makes you so sure?'

Hannah smiled. 'It's obvious to me when I see you together that you're both in love with each other. There can only be one conclusion—a happy ending.'

Tessa gave a wry smile. 'No offence, Hannah, but you make it sound like a romantic film. Real life's not like that. I don't think anybody can predict how it will end between us. We might stay together. On the other hand—' She stopped in mid-sentence as the door opened, holding her breath when she saw who it was. Had he heard anything?

'I didn't know you had a clinic today, Max,' Hannah said quickly.

'I haven't. I came to have a word with Tessa.'

Hannah smiled. 'Be my guest. I'll make myself scarce if—'

'Not that sort of word.' He was smiling now. 'This is work.'

He crossed the room and stood looking down at Tessa. 'I've just come down from Nightingale where I've been examining Josie Hargreaves. She told Staff Nurse Reeves she had backache. Her contractions have started so—'

'So we'll have to bring forward the Caesarean,' Tessa said quickly. 'We can't risk losing those triplets.'

'I remember Josie coming in for her antenatal appointments before she was admitted to Nightingale,' Hannah said. 'How far on is she now?'

'Josie is thirty-five weeks pregnant,' Max said. 'We'd

have preferred her to reach thirty-six because the triplets are still small, but with special care they should survive.'

He glanced at his watch and frowned.

'I'm on my way to Theatre now. Josie has asked if Tessa could assist with her Caesarean.'

'Yes, I'd like to be there,' Tessa said quickly.

'Of course you would,' Hannah said. 'Josie's a very special patient. Let me know what happens, won't you? I'll get Staff Nurse Phillips to give me a hand down here.'

Josie Hargreaves's tense face broke into a smile as she saw Tessa walking down the ward towards her bed.

'You came, Sister! They told me you were working in Outpatients this afternoon.'

Tessa smiled down at her patient. 'I was, but I came back as soon as I heard we were going to deliver you earlier than planned.'

Josie's face screwed up with pain. 'Little blighters are playing football. But it's never been as bad as this before.'

Tessa squeezed her hand. 'Not much longer.'

She scanned Josie's charts and saw that the pre-medication had already been given. It seemed to be taking effect because Josie was beginning to look sleepy.

'You've decided you want a general anaesthetic, haven't you, Josie?'

Josie nodded. 'Can't stand pain, Sister. I just want to go to sleep, wake up and have the babies given to me.'

'Would you like them gift-wrapped?'

Josie gave a sleepy smile. 'Yes, please. Pink ribbons if they're girls and blue bootees if they're boys, and, Sister...'

Tessa waited while Josie remembered what it was she was going to say.

'You'll be there, won't you, Sister? You and Mr Forster will make sure everything's OK, won't you?'

'Of course,' Tessa said. She pulled the curtains around the bed. 'Just relax and go to sleep.'

Josie's eyes were already closed. Good. Tessa couldn't help feeling a moment of apprehension about the impending operation. Suppose, just suppose there was some abnormality that hadn't been detected. It sometimes happened even in a super-efficient hospital like the Moortown General.

'I wonder if prize fighters feel like this when they're going into the ring?' Tessa said to Max as they scrubbed up together in the little anteroom next to the obstetrics theatre.

Max shook his hands dry and stood looking down at her with a quizzical expression while he waited for a theatre nurse to bring him some sterile gloves.

'Like what?'

'Well, nervous of the outcome for a start,' she admitted, her head down as she continued to scrub her nails.

'The only reason you're nervous is because you've become too involved with Josie,' Max said slowly. 'You've got to remain detached and completely professional about this case.'

'You find that easier than I do,' she said quietly.

A nurse had arrived with the gloves. Max waited until he was fitted and they were alone again, before replying.

'Look, Tessa, I can't think of anyone who assists me better in Theatre. But if you're going to be over-emotional about—'

'I'm not!'

She took a deep breath. 'I'm over it now. I'm completely ready for work…sir,' she added, her mouth crinkling into a smile behind her mask.

She could see he was smiling, too. His eyes above his mask held that indefinable expression of tenderness that she felt she could drown in.

'Besides, I promised the patient I'd check your every move…sir.'

He was stifling a laugh as the swing doors were opened for them by Theatre Sister.

'We're ready for you, sir.'

The babies were delivered in quick succession. As Max extricated the first one, a tiny little boy, through the incision he'd made in the wall of the womb, a collective sigh of relief went around the theatre.

'One down, two to go,' Max said, handing the slippery mite to Tessa, who proceeded to clear his airway and check his breathing.

Theatre Sister came forward to take the first baby away for postnatal checks and treatment, before placing him in an incubator.

In total, there were two boys and a girl, all perfectly healthy apart from being underweight.

'So you needn't have worried,' Max said quietly to Tessa as they watched a still-anaesthetised Josie being wheeled out of the theatre.

Tessa smiled happily. 'Three little bundles of joy for Josie. She'll be thrilled! I want to be there when she comes round.'

She raised her voice as she looked round at the nursing staff who were busily clearing up.

'Have we any blue bootees? Two pairs, if you've got them, please.'

Theatre Sister said she thought she could oblige.

'I've got some pink ribbon,' Tessa said thoughtfully, half to herself.

'What are you planning?' Max asked, following her into the ante room.

She threw her mask into the bin and looked up at him, smiling.

'A little celebration for Josie.'

'Well, don't get her too excited.'

'Now who's being over-anxious?' she quipped.

He gave her a wry grin. 'And what about after duty? Or are you planning to stay on the ward all night just to check that the night staff don't neglect your patients?'

He was standing very close now. They didn't have to remain sterile now that the operation was over. His theatre greens were touching hers. She gave an involuntary shiver of excitement as she looked up at him.

'What did you have in mind?'

He gave her a rakish grin as he placed both hands against her arms, and his expression was impossibly tender as he looked down at her.

'I've requested the weatherman to give us one of those warm June evenings that seem to go on for ever…or at least until the stars come out. I thought a game of tennis, a leisurely supper in the garden and then…who knows?'

She smiled, her excitement mounting at the promise of the wonderful evening ahead.

'You can't always win—at tennis, I mean,' she said quickly. 'I'm going to try really hard tonight.'

Slowly, he bent his head and kissed her gently on the mouth. 'I do hope so,' he whispered huskily.

CHAPTER NINE

SPRING had turned the corner into warm, dry summer—perfect for evening barbecues in Max's garden, long walks over the moors and swimming in the river together.

Tessa went over to see her family in Riversdale whenever she could find the time, but most of her off-duty time was spent with Max. Earlier on in their relationship she'd tried limiting their time together but it simply hadn't worked! Max was like a magnet, drawing her towards him. It was impossible to resist his charismatic personality.

At least, that was how she tried to rationalise it as she sat beside him on a hot July evening in Francesca's school hall, waiting for the curtain to rise on *Pride and Prejudice*, the end-of-term play. This occasion, in fact, was at Francesca's instigation, but she knew that Max was pleased she'd agreed to go with him.

He was leaning towards her. 'Isn't that Anne Reeves's husband going backstage?'

'He's in charge of the music tonight,' Tessa said.

'You mean he has to position the loudspeakers and put on the correct CD?' Max said, with pseudo-solemnity. 'Like he did at their wedding?'

She kept a straight face with difficulty. At Anne's and James's wedding reception in June Max had made a brief appearance, before persuading Tessa to escape for a long walk over the moors with him. He'd told her he couldn't stand wedding receptions with piped music in the background.

'Didn't Francesca tell you?' Tessa said. 'James teaches

music here. He wanted to arrange an orchestra to play an overture before the play but there wasn't enough support. Francesca said most of the musicians in the school orchestra were in the play.'

'No, Francesca didn't give me that little snippet of information. But, then, she talks to you more than she does to me nowadays. Is she still sulking because I won't buy the house and build a swimming pool?'

Tessa opened her eyes wide in mock innocence. 'I really couldn't say.'

Max pulled a wry face. 'No, I'm sure you couldn't! She'll come round sooner or later. It's probably her age. Does she talk to you about boyfriends and her periods and…well, whatever women talk about when they get together?'

Tessa smiled. 'Of course she does. But I'm not allowed to divulge any confidences.'

'Of course not… Look, there's Anne's husband coming this side of the curtain again. He looks pleased with himself.'

He paused and placed a hand over hers. 'At least you're not favouring Anne with extra off-duty time any more.'

'No, now that they're married I figured their relationship could slip into a steady decline like all marriages do,' she said, keeping her voice deliberately light.

In spite of her facetious tone, he looked surprised.

'Is that your own personal opinion of marriage or…?'

'No, of course it's not.'

She was watching his reaction very carefully now. 'But I thought it was yours. Shh, the curtain's rising.'

Before the lights dimmed she had time to see she'd set him thinking. Good!

Francesca was superb in her part of Elizabeth. Tessa's heart was bursting with pride as she and Max went backstage to congratulate her.

'You were wonderful,' Tessa said, kissing Francesca on her greasepainted cheek.

'Absolutely fabulous,' Max said.

They were surrounded by the excited cast and their proud parents.

'Are you and Mrs Forster going to stay for the party?' said a young, blonde woman, who, Tessa had gathered, was the drama teacher who'd produced the play.

'Sorry, we can't,' Max said quickly. 'Francesca's going to stay in Moortown with Joanna tonight after the party.'

He paused. 'Miss Thomson, this is my colleague at the hospital, Tessa Grainger.'

The drama teacher was trying to cover her obvious embarrassment.

'I just assumed…' She smiled, recovering some of her composure. 'I'm so pleased to meet you, Miss Grainger. Francesca is always talking about someone called Tessa. I assumed she was talking about one of her friends who lives in Cragdale.'

'Not far wrong. I live in Riversdale. I'm a friend of the family,' Tessa said quickly. 'Congratulations on putting on such an excellent play, Miss Thomson. It was first class.'

'Thank you. Couldn't do it without my students and the support of their parents—and friends,' she added quickly.

'Isn't that interesting that Miss Thomson really thought you were Francesca's mother,' Max said quietly, as he drove out of the school car park and headed towards Cragdale.

'Why shouldn't she? I was with her father and—'

'Yes, but I always thought I looked so much older than you.'

'Max, you make too much of this ten-year gap between us.'

'Yes, but when you're forty I'll be fifty, when I'm sixty you'll be only be fifty and…'

'So?'

They were stopped at traffic lights, waiting to turn right up the Cragdale road. For a moment while the car was stationary he looked at her, a long, searching look as if he'd never seen her before.

She held her breath. This talk of the future was terribly disturbing.

'The lights are changing, Max,' she prompted.

He drove forward.

'What if you decided to go off with a younger man?' he said quietly.

'Oh, Max, what is all this about?'

'Well, it happened to me once. It could happen again. I was always conscious of the fact that Catherine had missed her carefree youth by marrying at sixteen. I—'

He broke off in mid-sentence.

She was aware that he wanted to tell her something important, but the steep hill road was requiring his full concentration. She put her hand across and touched his arm.

'Catherine always looked pretty carefree when I saw her,' she said carefully. 'I don't think she missed out at all. Marriage didn't seem to put too many constraints on her.'

He remained silent, deep in thought as they crossed the moorland road, before negotiating the hairpin bends leading down into the valley.

It wasn't until they were safely inside the house, sitting beside each other on the sitting room sofa, that he brought up the subject of Catherine again.

'She may have looked carefree when you saw her, Tessa,' he said, topping up her wine glass with the bottle he'd brought in from the kitchen.

He put the bottle down on the little table beside the sofa and turned to look at her, a far-away expression in his eyes.

'Catherine was very good at hiding her feelings.'

He gave a loud sigh as he pulled her closer to him on the sofa.

She leaned her head against his shoulder and waited, hardly daring to breathe, intuitively sensing that he was about to make another revelation. It was important that he didn't lose his train of thought because she'd noticed in the past that each revelation seemed to bring them closer together.

She was still hoping for a revelation that would trigger a breakthrough in their relationship, the catalyst that would finally make Max recognise the possibilities of a permanent liaison with her.

'I was twenty-three when we married,' he said quietly.

She watched as he threw his head back and closed his eyes.

'Catherine was sixteen. I'd only known her six months…'

Silence for several seconds.

'Where did Catherine live?' Tessa asked to stimulate Max into continuing.

He opened his eyes again and looked at her with an enigmatic expression.

'She'd come up from London to spend a few weeks in Yorkshire with an aunt at the end of her summer term. She'd already left school and couldn't decide what she wanted to do so this holiday was supposed to be her decision time.'

'And you came along, and her future was decided?'

He smiled. 'Something like that. We met at one of those parties held by well-meaning relatives for young people to get to know each other. I was enticed over to Catherine's aunt's farm with a couple of other final-year medics on the promise of free food, free drink and a chance to meet some new talent.'

'Was it love at first sight?'

How could she bear to say that? She was trying so hard to cope with the jealous pangs that were sweeping over her when she thought of Max falling in love for the first time. But she had to hear him out.

'I think it was,' he said slowly.

'At the end of the evening I told her I'd like to see her again and she readily agreed. But by the end of the summer she was begging me to marry her, which was the last thing I wanted. I told her I'd like to wait but…but she said, "Let's get married as soon as possible or I'll go back to London and you'll never see me again".'

'It must have been hard, starting your medical career at the beginning of your marriage.'

'It was. Francesca was born ten months after our wedding. I was always busy at the hospital but I tried to make quality time when I was off duty.'

'Max, you did what you could. You found a babysitter, remember?'

He smiled down at her, ruffling her hair affectionately. 'One of the best moves I ever made. Little did I know all those years ago that we'd be sitting here like this… Now, where was I?'

'You were making quality time,' she prompted.

'I tried even harder when we went over to the States—to make quality time, I mean. But Catherine always wanted more than I could give. I was the one who suggested she join the health club, thinking it would keep her occupied during the day.'

'But that wasn't enough?'

'No. Then seven months before she died we found out she was pregnant.'

She put down her glass on the little side table. 'Max, I'd no idea that—'

'But at three months she had a miscarriage,' he went on in a flat voice. 'Her obstetrician, who was a friend of mine, advised her to wait at least a year before she tried to get pregnant again. The miscarriage had left her very weak.'

'So the miscarriage was only four months before she died?'

He nodded. 'I was very concerned about her health so I kept the promise I'd made to her obstetrician not to try for another baby until she was stronger. Catherine was very depressed after the miscarriage. Her vivacious personality changed completely but I wasn't prepared for what happened.'

'No, of course you weren't. It was—'

'I don't mean simply the way she died.'

He paused. 'I've never discussed this with anyone. I asked it to be hushed up at the autopsy.'

He swallowed hard.

She waited.

'The autopsy revealed that Catherine was six weeks pregnant when she died. We hadn't slept together since the miscarriage so this relationship with the swimming instructor had been going on for at least a few weeks.'

'Oh, Max!'

'She'd already turned to somebody else because she thought I was rejecting her. It was my fault that—'

'Max, it wasn't your fault. You're an obstetrician and a damn good one. You knew the complications that an early pregnancy after a miscarriage could cause. You took a conscious decision for Catherine's sake.'

For a few seconds he stared at her, his brow furrowed in deep concentration as the vivid memories receded.

'I never thought about it like that before,' he said quietly.

He pulled her closer, his lips seeking hers in a gentle kiss that grew more demanding as he felt her moulding herself against him, straining for more of his caresses.

'Let's go to bed,' he whispered, his voice urgent.

That night he made love to her with a newfound tenderness. She opened up with a deep sense of belonging. Max's revelations about Catherine seemed to have eased away the last of his tension. She sensed a new phase in their relationship had begun.

But in the morning, as she lay beside him, trying to keep still so that she wouldn't waken him, she wondered if Max had really experienced a permanent breakthrough.

Had he really accepted that none of Catherine's actions were his fault? Or was he still weighed down with the guilt that threatened to cripple his emotions and made it impossible for him to commit himself fully to a new relationship?

He stirred beside her. As soon as he opened his eyes he put out an arm and pulled her against him.

'I've been thinking,' he said, his lips nuzzling against her hair. 'Why don't you move in with me?'

She pulled herself away slightly so that she could look at him. She was very tempted by the idea but wary of the consequences of giving up some of her independence without any assurance of a permanent commitment.

She hesitated. 'I'm not sure. Give me some time to think about it.'

'What is there to think about? It's much more comfortable here than the nurses' home, isn't it?'

That was certainly true!

'My offer for Riverside cottage is still there,' she said slowly. 'When the owners manage to get possession of their new home I'll be able to—'

'If you were living here, you'd be able to move all your stuff straight down the valley. And I'd be able to help you.'

She could feel her spirits dropping. A temporary situation here was all that was on offer.

'I'll give the idea some thought,' she said quietly.

CHAPTER TEN

DURING the course of the summer there was a constant stream of ex-patients who came up to Nightingale to see Tessa. Sometimes their visits disrupted the work on the ward but she didn't mind. Patients, both past and present, were more important to her than routine.

On the hot September morning when Josie Hargreaves brought her triplets in to see Tessa all pretence at keeping the work going was stopped. Staff and patients alike gathered in the middle of the ward to drool over the three beautiful babies.

'They're nearly three months old,' Josie said proudly in answer to a query from one of the patients. 'My husband had this special buggy made for me so I can take them all out at once.'

Tessa looked down in amazement at the complicated contraption in which the three babies were comfortably snoozing.

'It looks as if you'd need a special driving licence to operate this, Josie,' Tessa said, walking around the buggy to get a better view. 'You're looking well.'

'Never better. Just had another postnatal check-up in Outpatients. Everything's fine with the babies and me.'

'Can I hold this one, Josie?' Anne Reeves asked.

'Of course.'

Josie was smiling proudly as she unlocked the complicated straps that held the baby in position. 'This is Adam.'

Tessa smiled as she watched her staff nurse. Anne had confided in Tessa only that morning that she'd just done a pregnancy test on herself and she was thrilled to announce that she was pregnant.

The maternal instinct was definitely showing as she took hold of the baby boy and held him against her.

Requests were now flooding in to hold the other babies and soon the entire trio were being passed around. The patients who were confined to bed were watching enviously, exhorting their ambulant friends to bring the babies over.

'Gently with the babies!' Tessa said, feeling like a mother hen as she followed the triplets around, ensuring that they were happy to be cuddled.

'So, what's this, a baby competition?'

She hadn't seen Max arriving. At the sound of his voice she looked up and smiled at him.

'These are the triplets we delivered in June. This one is Adam, here's Ian and this is Phoebe. Three little bundles of joy. Don't you think they're gorgeous?'

Max smiled. 'Wonderful! But very time-consuming, I would think.'

He was glancing at his watch. 'You've got a new patient for me to see, I believe, Sister.'

Tessa, who was now holding Adam, pointed out the bed where the new patient was getting herself settled in, aided by one of the nurses who'd been persuaded to do some work.

'I'll be with you in a minute when—'

'Don't worry, Sister. Staff Nurse will come with me. I don't want to break up the party.'

She glanced up at him and saw that his expression was one of fond amusement. Oh, well, if he was happy for Anne to assist him she'd be delighted to spend some more time with the babies.

Her relationship with Max had reached what she could only think of as an indeterminate stage. In a sense they were both watching and waiting for the other one to make the next move.

Max had asked her to come and live with him at Oak Cottage but she hadn't taken up the offer. He hadn't tried to press the issue. She still spent occasional idyllic nights over at his house in Cragdale but there was a definite air of constraint in the mornings.

The fact that she still had to pack up her things and go back to the nurses' home was an unacknowledged bone of contention. Max obviously couldn't see why she was hesitating over his suggestion, whereas she was still unwilling to move in without some indication from him that this wasn't simply going to be a temporary arrangement.

She glanced down at the baby boy in her arms. His little rosebud mouth puckered into a smile.

'You're absolutely perfect, Adam,' she whispered, 'but I'd better give you back to your mum and get on with some work.'

When she finally managed to persuade her staff and patients to relinquish their hold on the triplets and resume their morning routine, she walked to the door with Josie.

'Come back and see us again, Josie,' she said, as she helped the proud mother to negotiate the buggy between the swing doors and out into the corridor.

'Thanks for everything, Sister. You've been great…right from the start and all the way through.'

Tessa had a lump in her throat as she watched Josie pushing the buggy down the corridor.

'Another satisfied customer,' Max said, taking the weight of the heavy swing doors from Tessa. 'Now, do you think you could possibly spare me a few minutes to discuss this new patient's treatment, Sister?'

She raised an eyebrow. 'Over a cup of coffee?'

He smiled down at her with that heart-rending expression that always made her pulses race.

'Why not?'

They talked at some length about the new case, Tessa jotting down notes as she made the coffee. Their new patient, Pam Asquith, was expecting twins, conceived after fertility treatment. Apparently, this was her third attempt and they were hoping it would be successful.

'I'll give her priority care,' Tessa said, putting down her cup of coffee. 'There's no need to worry, Max. This morning was a one-off situation. I'm usually very organised but when my ex-patients bring in the fruits of our labours—'

She broke off and smiled. 'I suppose that should be the fruit of their labour, shouldn't it? They're the ones who do most of the work.'

'But they couldn't do without us, could they, Tessa?'

'Not in these high-tech days they couldn't. All these multiple pregnancies make obstetrics very complicated. I don't know if I'd have the patience to go through with all the treatment some of our patients endure if I were infertile.'

'I'm sure you'd find the patience from somewhere…but let's hope you never need to find out,' he said quietly.

She remained very still. He was watching her with a mixture of tenderness and professional pride.

Come on, Max, she wanted to say. Put your cards on the table, for God's sake!

But he remained silent, not knowing that her every nerve was tuned in to his slightest remark. Oh, well, if that was the end of the conference she was going to get back to her patients.

She stood up. 'I'll go and see Pam Asquith.'

'Will you come over this afternoon?' she heard him say in a matter-of-fact voice.

He was so sure of himself.

'I know you've given yourself a long weekend, starting this afternoon,' he continued with a wry grin, ''cos I looked on the Nightingale duty roster. I don't know what you're planning but…'

'I'm planning to go over to the farm at some point to see Mum.'

'You could do that tomorrow or Sunday. Why not come over to the cottage this afternoon? It's a glorious day out there and we can't be sure how long this good weather will hold. How about one last swim in the river before September gets into its usual mood?'

'You mean there's nothing like a refreshing swim on a hot day?'

He reached forward and put a finger under her chin, tilting her face so that she had to look into his eyes.

'You can go over to Riversdale in the morning, can't you?'

'You've got the sort of expression that would melt an iceberg!' She smiled up at him.

He grinned. 'See you this afternoon…'

As she walked off down the ward she reflected that when she'd first started staying over at Max's house he'd always reminded her to bring her toothbrush. Her one concession to their sleeping arrangement had been to leave a toothbrush in Max's bathroom cupboard.

But that was all. She still had her independence even if it was a bit dented.

'This water's still cold even after our long, hot summer,' she called, striking out towards Max who was already treading water as he waited for her in the middle of the river.

'It never warms up,' he shouted. 'It's flowing too quickly.'

She joined him and for a few moments they trod water

together. The current was beginning to carry them down-stream.

'Let's swim upstream first,' Tessa said. 'Get the hard bit out of the way while we're still fresh and then we can let the river float us back again.'

'Good idea!'

She felt very safe with Max at her side as she swam upstream. She knew he could go much faster than she could but he always chose to stay with her. If she needed to catch her breath he trod water with her, only resuming his strokes when she did.

'That's far enough,' she called as she felt herself tiring. 'Now for the easy bit!'

It was such fun to glide back with the current of the river pulling her along.

'I love the homeward stretch,' she called above the rushing of the river.

Turning over, she completed the last section doing back-stroke. Looking up at the blue sky with only a hint of white, fluffy cloud, she thought how wonderful it would be if she and Max could go on living like this for ever.

He put out a hand and hauled her up the steep river bank. She lay down on the towel she'd spread in the sun before they'd started out. Max was lying on his towel, his sun-tanned body almost touching hers.

'I can just make out the beginning of the garden around your cottage through the trees further down the river, Tessa. Look!'

She rolled onto her side, supporting herself on her elbow.

'If only it was my cottage. I made a phone call to the owners only yesterday and they're still caught up in a house chain. They apologised for keeping me waiting but said there was nothing they could do until the house they're buying becomes vacant.'

'You've been very patient.'

'That's what the estate agent said when I phoned him after speaking to the owners. He pointed out that there were other properties on the market if I wanted a quicker move. Apparently, somebody has made a higher offer for Riverside Cottage but the owners are doing the honourable thing by holding it for me.'

'And do you want a quicker move?'

'None of the other properties are in Cragdale, and that's where I've set my heart on living.'

'Good! I wasn't sure that Cragdale was where you really wanted to live. I'll fax my offer for Oak Cottage as soon as we get back.'

She was totally perplexed. 'Max, I thought we were talking about me buying a cottage, not you.'

'The owners of Oak Cottage faxed me to say they're not coming back here from the Far East. They're going to put it on the market if I'm not interested in buying. And I'm only interested in buying if you don't want to move from Cragdale.'

'Why on earth would I want to move from Cragdale? I love the place.'

'And it hasn't got unhappy memories for you?' He paused. 'I mean, its association with Catherine…and the fact that Cragdale was where we lived when we were first married?'

'I've only got happy memories of Catherine,' she said carefully.

She didn't mention the fact that from everything she'd learned she'd formed quite a different opinion of Catherine to the one she'd had as a naïve, sixteen-year-old babysitter.

He seemed relieved. 'Well, that's another of the obstacles out of the way. I suspected that this prolonged wait to move into your cottage might be because you were deciding whether you still wanted to live in Cragdale or not—I mean, after all the harrowing revelations I've given you concerning Catherine.'

'Max…what exactly…?'

'In that case, I think you should tell the estate agent to accept the higher offer from the other client,' he said briskly.

'Max, you've got me totally…'

He moved closer to her, reaching out to take both her hands in his.

'I know you'll plead for time to think about this but, Tessa…will you marry me?'

He held up a hand as she half opened her mouth to reply.

'No, don't answer until you've given it some thought. I'm prepared to be patient but please don't keep me in suspense for too long.'

Her heart was turning over and over as she waited for a chance to speak.

'Yes, I'll marry you.'

She paused for a few seconds because her voice was cracking with emotion. Max, she noticed, was gazing down at her with eyes that were decidedly moist. He was uncharacteristically lost for words.

She cleared her throat. 'But what did you mean just now when you said that was another obstacle out of the way?'

He took a deep breath, his fingers tightening on hers.

'There were reasons why I shied away from marriage. After Catherine died I felt I couldn't live at that level of emotional intensity again. I kept a tight rein on my emotions. But that changed when I was with you. My normal feelings returned, but I felt I wouldn't be able to stand it if you left me for someone else.'

'That's the once-bitten-twice-shy syndrome,' Tessa said gently. 'But, Max, that simply wouldn't happen.'

'That's what you told me that time when we were discussing the disparity in our ages. That was another obstacle in the path. I felt reassured after you'd told me the age difference didn't matter to you.'

He pulled her against him. 'And I reasoned that you might think marriage would be too big a step for you to take after such a short relationship with me. And I didn't want to rush into marriage like I did last time. We've got a whole lifetime ahead of us so there was no reason for a quick marriage.'

'So what's changed?'

'Step by step, I've become convinced that you want to stay with me so marriage is the obvious conclusion.'

'Not the conclusion, the beginning,' she said quietly, feeling mounting excitement at the thought of this new adventure. Ahead of her were years and years of life with Max beside her.

He was smiling now in a decidedly boyish sort of way. 'I can't believe this is for real!'

She laughed. 'Neither can I!'

He kissed her gently on the lips. She responded to his deepening kiss until he pulled away and hauled her to her feet.

'We'll be much more comfortable in the house,' he said, his voice husky with the promise of what was to come.

'You've got that important fax to send,' she said.

He put his finger against her lips. 'Shh! Stop being so practical. I'll send the fax afterwards. And then I'll phone the builders and ask them to start work on the swimming pool. They've already given me an estimate.'

She stared at him. 'So you intended to stay after all!'

He gave her a wry grin. 'I just wanted to make sure that I wouldn't be alone in my old age before I went ahead. I didn't want to burn my boats until I'd talked you round.'

They gathered up their towels and ran barefoot, laughing together as they skipped over the warm pebbles that were scattered amongst the springy grass, and she wondered, fleetingly, whether she should confess that she hadn't needed any persuasion. If only he'd told her his reasons for holding off sooner!

But as they neared her future home, nestling amid the oak trees, she reflected that there were some things that were best left unsaid.

Or, as her father who was Yorkshire born and bred used to advise, least said, soonest mended.

Max squeezed her hand as he pulled her to a halt. Francesca could be seen running towards them through the open gate at the bottom of the garden.

'I've been looking for you everywhere. Joanna's mum is waiting for me in the car. Can I stay with them tonight? Joanna's got to babysit her little brother and— Hey, what's happened?'

'Nothing's happened. Well…'

Max was trying to temper his besotted smile as he turned to look at Tessa, his eyes beseeching her to give him some help.

'Francesca,' Tessa started, wondering how you announced the most important piece of news in the world to a young, vulnerable girl. 'We've got something to tell you…'

'Don't tell me Dad's decided to build the swimming pool?'

Tessa laughed. 'How did you guess?'

'But if he's going to build the swimming pool…then that means we're going to stay here. And there can only be one reason for that. Oh, Tessa!'

Francesca flung her arms round Tessa at the same time that Max put his arms round both of them.

'I knew Dad would come to his senses and see what was

staring him in the face.' Francesca sighed, happily. 'Can I be a bridesmaid?'

'That goes without saying,' Tessa told her.

Francesca glanced first at Tessa and then at Max. 'So you won't mind if I make myself scarce this evening?'

Max pulled a pained face. 'We'll force ourselves to cope without you.'

Francesca giggled. 'I bet you will. Congratulations, the pair of you.'

They made love in the wide four-poster bed in a languid, unhurried manner, as if both of them wanted to relish the fact that a whole new world had been opened up to them.

Tessa had never imagined she could experience such ecstasy as she lay in Max's arms, knowing that she would be with him for the rest of her life.

Later, much later, they put on their dressing-gowns and went down into the kitchen in search of some supper. Their wet swimsuits were still lying on the floor where they'd torn them off in their haste to reach the bedroom.

Max reached inside the fridge and pulled out a bottle of champagne.

'I'm starving,' Tessa said, opening a carton of eggs. 'Do you like omelettes?'

'So the lady can cook? That's great! I didn't know.'

'There's a lot you don't know about me,' Tessa said. 'But we've got a whole lifetime to get to know each other. Where's the egg whisk? Ah, here it is.'

The champagne cork flew across the kitchen. Tessa laughed as she watched Max searching for it on the floor.

'This is a special cork. I'm going to keep this as a memento,' he said, depositing it in the pocket of his robe. 'The day I proposed to the most wonderful woman in the world.'

'And she accepted...for better, for worse, for—'

'It's going to be for better,' he said, handing her a glass. 'Here's to the next hundred years together!'

Tessa giggled as the bubbles flew up her nose. 'I'll be a hundred and thirty.'

'And I'll only be a hundred and forty so…'

'Oh, don't start that again, Max!'

EPILOGUE

'OF COURSE I don't mind babysitting,' Francesca said. 'Actually, I've invited a friend for supper.'

Tessa smiled. 'Oh, good. Anyone I know?'

'It's Steve.' Francesca pushed back her chair from the kitchen table and stood up. 'I've got to go and phone him now to confirm.'

'Who's Steve?' Max asked.

Tessa put her hand on Francesca's arm. 'Not the fantastic Steve who appeared after you'd thrown the apple peel over your shoulder?'

Francesca grinned. 'The very same.'

Edward banged his spoon impatiently on the food tray attached to his high chair.

Max was looking decidedly puzzled as he leaned forward to put another spoonful of scrambled egg into Edward's open mouth.

'What on earth are you talking about?'

Tessa laughed. 'You've got a short memory, Max. Don't you remember Francesca talking about Hallowe'en night when she threw a piece of apple peel over her shoulder and it formed the shape of an S?'

Edward tossed his spoon on the floor and started to protest loudly at the lack of attention he was getting from the grown-ups. Tessa moved her chair nearer to their baby son and took over the feeding from Max.

'You must remember, Dad,' Francesca said. 'I told you that I'd met this fantastic boy at the school disco. He bought me a Coca-Cola. I didn't see him again for ages and then...'

Max ran a hand through his hair. 'Yes, now you mention it…but that must be more than three years ago. It was one of the first times Tessa came here for supper.'

Edward had eaten enough breakfast and was decidedly restless now as he strained against the straps holding him into his chair. Tessa wiped his sticky face and hands and lifted him onto her lap.

'We were all sitting round the table here and I peeled an apple, which started Francesca talking about Steve,' Tessa said, cradling Edward in her arms.

Edward rewarded her with a wide smile, displaying his two new teeth. 'Mum, mum, mum…'

'I'll go upstairs and make that phone call,' Francesca said.

Max gave his daughter a knowing grin. 'What's wrong with the kitchen phone?'

Francesca was smiling as she hurried out of the kitchen.

'Doesn't seem as if it's more than three years since you first came here,' Max said.

He picked up the cafetière. 'Would you like more coffee?'

Edward was struggling to be released again. Tessa put him down on the floor, where he proceeded to crawl under the table. Finding the spoon he'd thrown earlier, he banged it against the table leg, making what was obviously a pleasing sound to his ears.

'Yes, please.'

Tessa held out her cup towards Max. 'We've packed a lot into that three years.'

'They've been the happiest years of my life,' Max said, his voice husky as he leaned across the table to grasp Tessa's hand.

She swallowed hard. 'That's a lovely thing to say to a girl on her second wedding anniversary.' She paused. 'Where are you taking me tonight?'

He smiled. 'Big secret! Posh restaurant, but I won't tell you which. Will you wear that cream silk suit you wore when you first came for supper? It's got such happy memories.'

'If I can still get into it. I've put on a bit of weight since I had Edward.'

'Nonsense! You're still beautifully slim. A bit plumper round the bosom maybe but you needed that when you were breast-feeding.'

Edward, tiring of the spoon and table game, was now crawling over to the saucepan stand. Taking the first one he could grasp at ground level, he banged it loudly on the floor.

Tessa went across, picked him up and carried him over to his toy corner. As soon as he was fully occupied with his building bricks she went back to the table.

'I love these summer mornings when everything's fresh,' she said, looking across the kitchen at the open window. 'It was a lovely day like this two years ago. Do you remember the smell of the roses that Mum had arranged in Cragdale church for our wedding?'

'I only remember waiting at the altar for the most beautiful girl in the world. And when she arrived by my side, all mysterious with a veil over her face, I remember thinking that this was the happiest moment of my life…but I was wrong.'

'What do you mean?'

'There have been moments far happier since then. The moment that Edward gave his first cry and…'

She smiled. 'And I was squeezing your hand so tightly at the end of my labour that you had bruised fingers for days!'

'I said our life would get better, didn't I? That day when we'd been swimming and I proposed to you?'

She nodded, her heart too full for words. It had been a

wonderful two years and nine months since that warm September day.

She'd moved into Oak Cottage immediately and they'd been married the following June. They'd taken their time over the wedding preparations. There had been no reason to rush.

Tessa's mother had been over the moon with joy and had insisted on masterminding what she'd intended to be the wedding of the year. And it had been a fabulous occasion. It seemed as if the entire staff of Moortown General had been over in Cragdale that day. Even the weather had favoured them with glorious June sunshine.

She remembered her mother commenting on the fact that they didn't need the marquee after all. The huge tent had been erected in the field nearest the farm in case of rain, but it had been so hot inside it that the caterers had been persuaded to move all the tables and chairs outside and erect parasols to shield the sun.

Max had contacted his parents at their house in Greece and had been amazed when they'd insisted on coming over for the wedding and staying at Oak Cottage to be with Francesca when Tessa and Max had flown off for their honeymoon in Italy. According to Max, his parents had definitely mellowed since their retirement.

Francesca, delighted to meet her grandparents, had gone back to Greece with them at the end of term and had stayed for most of the summer holidays. That had meant that Tessa and Max had been alone for those first idyllic weeks of their marriage.

'When we celebrated our first wedding anniversary I certainly couldn't get into my silk suit,' she joked.

'You looked wonderful, even six months pregnant... especially six months pregnant.'

Tessa glanced at the grandfather clock. 'Max, you're going to be very late if you don't go now. I thought you had a long theatre list today?'

He stood up, smiling ruefully down at her. 'I have. And I'm taking Francesca in to observe surgical procedures.'

'Do you find it difficult, having Francesca at the hospital as a first-year medical student?'

'Not really. She's mostly in lectures at this early stage. This theatre visit is a one-off so...' He paused. 'I wonder if the fantastic Steve is a medical student. Come to think of it, I did see her talking very animatedly to a young man when I picked her up outside the medical school yesterday.'

'Max, you'd better go.'

Tessa stood up so that he could put his arms around her before he kissed her goodbye. His kiss was still infinitely exciting, still wonderfully arousing, but she was trying to stay sane and sensible. There were hours before they could make love again.

Remembering the night they'd just spent together, she shivered in his arms.

'I'm looking forward to tonight,' she whispered.

'So am I.' His arms tightened around her. 'Sure you still like being at home? Not missing Nightingale?'

She looked up at him. 'Sometimes I miss the excitement of hospital, but then I look at Edward and know this is where I want to be. In a few years maybe I'll think about going back.'

'In a few years maybe you'll be too busy with the other children to.'

She smiled. 'So how many others are we planning?'

'Let's discuss it tonight...when we're alone...after our anniversary supper...'

MILLS & BOON®

*M*akes
any time
special

Enjoy a romantic novel from
Mills & Boon®

Presents...™   *Enchanted*™   *Temptation*®

Historical Romance™   *Medical Romance*™

MILLS & BOON®

MEDICAL ROMANCE™

HER PASSION FOR DR JONES by Lilian Darcy
Southshore - No.1 of 4

Dr Harry Jones is sure it's a mistake having Rebecca Irwin work in the practice. Despite the raging attraction between her and Harry, Rebecca fought her corner!

BACHELOR CURE by Marion Lennox
Bachelor Doctors

Dr Tessa Westcott burst into Mike Llewellyn's life like a red-headed whirlwind. She said exactly what she thought, and turned his ordered world upside down. It couldn't last. But Mike had to admit, she lightened his life.

HOLDING THE BABY by Laura MacDonald

Lewis's sister was abroad and he was left holding the baby—literally! He *badly* needed help with the three children and asked Jo Henry to be nanny. In a family situation, Jo and Lewis became *vividly* aware of each other...

SEVENTH DAUGHTER by Gill Sanderson

Specialist registrar Dr James Owen was everything Dr Delyth Price ever wanted in a man. But Delyth had a gift not everyone understood. James seemed prepared to listen, if not to believe. Then she discovered his lighthearted side, and fell even deeper into love...

Available from 3rd September 1999

MILLS & BOON®

Next Month's Romance Titles

$\heartsuit$

Each month you can choose from a wide variety of romance novels from Mills & Boon®. Below are the new titles to look out for next month from the Presents...™ and Enchanted™ series.

Presents...™

A BOSS IN A MILLION	Helen Brooks
HAVING LEO'S CHILD	Emma Darcy
THE BABY DEAL	Alison Kelly
THE SEDUCTION BUSINESS	Charlotte Lamb
THE WEDDING-NIGHT AFFAIR	Miranda Lee
REFORM OF THE PLAYBOY	Mary Lyons
MORE THAN A MISTRESS	Sandra Marton
THE MARRIAGE EXPERIMENT	Catherine Spencer

Enchanted™

TYCOON FOR HIRE	Lucy Gordon
MARRYING MR RIGHT	Carolyn Greene
THE WEDDING COUNTDOWN	Barbara Hannay
THE BOSS AND THE PLAIN JAYNE BRIDE	Heather MacAllister
THE RELUCTANT GROOM	Emma Richmond
READY, SET...BABY	Christie Ridgway
THE ONE-WEEK MARRIAGE	Renee Roszel
UNDERCOVER BABY	Rebecca Winters

On sale from 3rd September 1999

H1 9908

Available at most branches of WH Smith, Tesco, Asda, Martins, Borders, Easons, Volume One/James Thin and most good paperback bookshops

Spoil yourself next month
with these four novels from

TEMPTATION.

MACKENZIE'S WOMAN by JoAnn Ross

Bachelor Auction

Kate Campbell had to persuade Alec Mackenzie to take part in a
charity bachelor auction. This rugged adventurer would have
women bidding millions for an hour of his time. Trouble was,
Alec wasn't really a bachelor. Though nobody knew it—he was
married to Kate!

A PRIVATE EYEFUL by Ruth Jean Dale

Hero for Hire

Nick Charles was a bodyguard on a vital assignment. But no one
had yet told him exactly what that assignment was! So he was
hanging around a luxury resort, waiting… Then along came
luscious Cory Leblanc and Nick just knew she was a prime
candidate—for *something*…

PRIVATE LESSONS by Julie Elizabeth Leto

Blaze

'Harley' turned up on Grant Riordan's doorstep and sent his
libido skyrocketing. Hired as the 'entertainment' for a bachelor
party, she was dressed like an exotic dancer but had the eyes of
an innocent. Unfortunately, after a little accident, she didn't
have a clue who she was…

SEDUCING SYDNEY by Kathy Marks

Plain-Jane Sydney Stone was feeling seriously out of place in a
glamorous Las Vegas hotel, when she received a mysterious
note arranging a date—for that night! She was sure the message
must have been delivered to the wrong woman. But maybe
she'd just go and find out…

ARE YOU A FAN
OF MILLS & BOON®
MEDICAL ROMANCES™?

If YOU are a regular United Kingdom buyer of Mills & Boon Medical Romances we would welcome your opinion on the books we publish.

Harlequin Mills & Boon have a Reader Panel for Medical Romances. Each person on the panel receives a questionnaire every third month asking for their opinion of the books they have read in the past three months. Everyone who sends in their replies will have a chance of winning ONE YEAR'S FREE Medicals, sent by post—48 books in all.

If you would like to be considered for inclusion on the Panel please give us details about yourself below. All postage will be free. Younger readers are particularly welcome.

Year of birth.............................Month...........................

Age at completion of full-time education......................

Single ❏   Married ❏   Widowed ❏   Divorced ❏

Your name (print please)...

Address..

....Postcode ....

Thank you! Please put in envelope and post to:
HARLEQUIN MILLS & BOON READER PANEL,
FREEPOST SF195, PO BOX 152, SHEFFIELD S11 8TE

THE
Regency
COLLECTION

Where rogues find romance

Look out for the fifth volume in this limited collection of Regency Romances from Mills & Boon® in September.

Featuring:

My Lady Love
by Paula Marshall

and

Four in Hand
by Stephanie Laurens

Still only £4.99

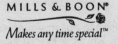

MILLS & BOON®

Makes any time special™